See Paris Before "I Do"

A Simone Simpson Mystery

Rita Smircich

See Paris Before "I Do"

A Simone Simpson Mystery

Rita Smircich

Published by "I Do" LLC

Cover design by Chris Murphy: www.cmurph.com
Book design by Pamela Pitcher: pam@documentclarity.com

Paperback ISBN: 978-1-7335014-1-5
Second Edition

Printed in the United States of America 2019

Author's Note:

This is a work of fiction.
Names, characters, places, and incidents either
are the products of my imagination or are used
factiously, and any resemblance to actual persons,
living or dead, business establishments, events
or locals is entirely coincidental.

Special thanks to Judith Marks-White, whose encouragement helped me find my literary voice. Her patience, teachings and friendship are the building blocks to this book.

Thank you to my friend, Laurie Goldberg for her technology knowledge, patience and advice. Without her, the final steps of getting this work published would have never happened.

Thank you to Kimberly, Ed, Pam, my family and friends for their continued support.

Dedication:

*This book is dedicated to Cathédrale Notre-Dame de Paris.
How does a writer, who created scenes that included the Cathedral, move forward with her work? This book was written before the destructive fire that took place on April 15, 2019. It is with deep sadness and hope that Cathédrale Notre-Dame de Paris will rise from the ashes, and once again be an iconic and welcoming home of worship.*

One

"Violated. I feel violated," Simone Simpson cried to Sargent Franco.

"Tell me again, when was it you discovered the items missing?" he asked, as his pen hovered over a pocket notebook.

"You've asked me three times. And each time I've told you the same thing: last night my partner, Jennifer Keys and I landed at LaGuardia Airport at ten-fifteen. Car service dropped me off at eleven forty-five. Then, he continued on and drove Jennifer home. It was late. I was tired. I dropped my bags, washed my face, and went to sleep."

"Then what happened?" the officer asked.

Sounding exasperated, she continued, "I woke up at six-thirty. I took a shower, then tried to assemble my outfit for the day. That's when I noticed all my underwear missing. Left behind was a sachet of dried lavender. Even the underwear in my hamper was stolen."

"Can you describe your . . . ahem . . . underwear?" the officer asked awkwardly.

"You're kidding, right?" Simone snapped, impatience and embarrassment taking over.

A tall African-American policewoman with large brown eyes approached. "May I help, Ms. Simpson?" Extending her hand, she gave Simone a firm, solid handshake. "I'm Police Chief Cindy Jacobs."

She turned to the policeman and said, "Franco, I'll take it from here."

Avoiding the woman's eyes, he responded, "Yes, ma'am."

"Ms. Simpson, I'm sorry this has happened. I overheard you tell Officer Franco that you discovered your underwear missing this morning, after being away on business. The officers will dust for prints, take some photographs, and be out of your way shortly."

Simone looked around at her bedroom, a sense of violation surfacing again.

The Police Chief locked eyes with Simone, and asked, "Can you think of anyone who might have come in while you were away? Have you had any workmen here, a dog walker, or someone picking up your mail?"

Simone shook her head 'no.' She needed coffee to clear her muddled mind. "I can't think of anyone. As far as I can recall, no one has a key, other than Cynthia, my next door neighbor, and my housekeeper." She added quickly before the Chief could ask more questions, "And please, call me Simone."

The woman did not extend the same casual offer. Instead, she maintained her professional demeanor. "Maybe the neighbor thought your plants needed watering, and sent someone in to do the job."

"Look around - I don't have any plants because I travel a lot."

"How about a boyfriend?"

"He doesn't have a key to my house," Simone said flatly.

Simone walked into her living room, away from the upsetting activity taking place in her master bedroom. There, more policemen were taking notes, and dusting the doorframe and doorknob for prints. She turned and headed towards the kitchen. "Coffee. I need coffee," she mumbled to herself, as if a cup of the brown elixir would erase her troubles.

Snarky remarks about her missing panties weren't concealed by the chatter of police radios. The Chief glared at them. The men scattered, going back to their duties. Jacobs followed Simone to the kitchen, and over the whirl of the brewing machine, tried lightening the mood. "Simone, between you and me, I think this is a good excuse to go shopping."

Simone forced a smile. The Chief didn't know if it was because of what she had just said, or from the intense aroma emanating from Simone's oversized coffee mug.

"I'm sorry, Chief. Would you like a cup?" Simone asked after swallowing her first sip perfectly prepared with half and half.

"No, no thanks," she answered. Her words said no, but the Chief's eyes lingered on the coffee. Simone could have sworn the woman licked her lips, like a starving man drooling over a perfectly cooked steak. The Chief forced her eyes away from the temptation and focused on Simone. "Is there anything else missing?"

"No, not that I can see. But, as I go about my daily routine, I'll let you know if I discover anything else missing. Thank you, Chief Jacobs. I'm glad you could cut the tension back there," she said as she tilted her head towards her bedroom. "I know you said your officers will be here a bit longer, but I need to get to work." Her words trailed off as she took the last gulps of coffee. She wanted to leave, go back to work, and make believe this never happened.

"Twenty minutes at the most. Meanwhile, here's my card. Call me anytime, even if you think it's unimportant. We'd rather have a false alarm than a tragedy. Consider getting security cameras installed. You can monitor your home from your cell phone. And don't forget to change your locks."

Simone nodded, not processing the suggestions, as her thoughts drifted toward a second cup of coffee. A caffeine-deprived headache continued to brew at the base of her skull.

"It's been our experience that you not mention this event to anyone. You never know, the perpetrator might be someone close to you."

"What about my neighbor, Cynthia? Will you tell her my underwear was stolen?"

The Chief smiled. "Don't worry, we won't tell her the details. We'll just say you discovered something missing from your home, and ask if she's seen anyone suspicious on your property."

Finally, the blue uniforms left her house. She was alone to confront feelings of violation and invasion. *I'm not going to get anything accomplished by feeling sorry for myself,* she thought. She filled her to-go mug with another cup of coffee, packed up her messenger bag, and headed out to accomplish errands.

While she drove, she reflected on possible suspects. Her housekeeper, Anna Maria worked for her for two years. Simone had never found anything missing, or out of place, and Anna Maria had many opportunities. In fact, if she found an errant earring or necklace, Anna Maria would place it on the kitchen counter with a note stating where she found the item.

She considered Cynthia. She was the first person to welcome Simone to the neighborhood. She worked as a teacher at the local high school, and her husband was an attorney in town. Their son mowed

Simone's lawn, did odd-jobs for her, and was going off to college in a few weeks. He was a responsible and respectful young man. Simone dismissed Cynthia and her family from the list of suspects.

Shortly after buying her home in Westport, Cynthia and her husband hosted an informal cookout on Compo Beach, and invited Simone. There, she was introduced to the other neighbors and, in particular, Pete Cody, a contractor. It didn't take Simone and Pete long to figure out they had been set up.

Simone found Pete interesting, engaging, and very attractive. He had a contagious laugh that started in the depths of his stomach and infected everyone around him. Standing well over six feet, his muscular arms strained against the sleeves of his pale-blue fitted polo shirt that matched his eyes. Dark chest hairs peaked out from the unbuttoned collar. He had a day-old scruffy beard. Simone was smitten.

He found Simone exciting, beautiful, sexy, and impressed that she had purchased the "old Raymo" house.

"I'd raise the house to avoid damage from hurricanes, put a two-car garage underneath, and add French doors leading to a deck. Although you're near the water, the humidity gets high in the northeast, so I'd recommend central air." His eyes drifted up to the sky, as if seeing the image before him. He continued, "I'd create a large master suite, with a custom-built bed that sits high on a platform, giving you a bird's eye view of the sunrise and the crashing waves." His eyes drifted back to Simone's. He paused, grinned slightly and added, "It's a great way to wake up, don't you think?"

Simone was speechless, mesmerized by his voice and vision. She wondered if his question had a double meaning.

Breaking the spell, he added, "And I'll introduce you to my landscape architect who can design a Zen garden."

Simone was intrigued how he would transpose the old neglected house into an updated structure. The longer they talked, the more she liked his ideas. And the greater their attraction grew.

Two days later she called Pete and hired him to do the renovations. She wasn't interested in having her bed up on a platform, but all the other suggestions were to her liking. He promised to construct a stunning, updated shabby-chic beach cottage. The project commenced, as well as their mutual attraction to each other. They spent many hours discussing ideas, reviewing architectural drawings, shopping for appliances, cabinets, and fixtures. The long days were often followed by dinner that quickly segued into weekends together.

They explored the Berkshires. They sat in oversized rocking chairs on the patio of Stockbridge's Red Lion Inn where they lingered over frozen Daiquiris, listened to classical music at Tanglewood in Lenox, and purchased books for Simone's library at Yellow House Books in Great Barrington.

Pete owned a cottage in Old Saybrook, Connecticut. Together, they spent long, lazy days by the water, kayaking, swimming or lounging under a large umbrella. At night they enjoyed the abundance of fresh seafood, and a late-night stroll on the private beach attached to his cottage.

It was a glorious, relaxing summer.

After six months, the renovations were completed and Simone was thrilled with the results. Pete's stay over weekends morphed into a few nights during the week, and then, for weeks at a time. He never expressed a desire to return to his own home.

Their relationship was moving too quickly for Simone. *Maybe it's my fault,* she thought. *I should not have been so available.* Pete moved their relationship from dating to living together in a matter of a few months. She enjoyed being with Pete, but she realized, she wasn't in love with him.

It had been nine months since she moved to Westport after living with Mr. and Mrs. Smith in Charlottesville. The Smiths had taken her in after her husband's untimely death, and helped her move from Tribeca to their Virginia home. They were more family to her than her own brother, with whom she hadn't spoken in several years following her parents' death.

Simone was looking forward to enjoying her new home. Alone. She needed to forge a life as an independent woman.

"Pete, we need to talk," she said one evening. "How do you see our relationship evolving? It seems you've moved into my home, and we never discussed living together."

"I thought you were comfortable with that," he responded. And without taking a breath between words, he rambled, "I like living with you. Maybe we'll get married in the next year, and start a family."

"Whoa!" Simone exclaimed jumping up from her sofa, suddenly feeling trapped. "Don't you think you're moving too quickly? I've just moved here, and I wasn't prepared to go directly into a serious relationship, no less get married and have children right away." Simone walked into the kitchen and refilled her wine glass. Her heart pounded as her thoughts scrambled between not wanting to hurt Pete's feelings, to protecting her heart, to a slight sense of dread of being alone once again. Pete remained quiet.

She returned to the sofa, and took his hand. "I'm sorry if I've hurt your feelings, Pete. I enjoy being with you . . . I really do . . . it's just that I'm not ready for such a serious commitment."

"I guess I moved too quickly," Pete said. "I want to get married and have kids. Lots of kids. Don't you?"

Simone pondered, realizing he wasn't the man with whom she wanted to have children. He was smart and sexy, but she couldn't see a "until death do us part" relationship. Neither one had ever professed their love for each other.

"I do want to get married again, but not right now," was all Simone could mutter. She held back tears as her thoughts flashed to her husband, Joe, and their unborn baby, lost in an instant on that tragic night years ago.

The next morning, Pete moved his belongings back to his home. Their intimate relationship fizzled out, just as quickly as it had started. They promised each other to remain friends. It was a vow they kept and honored without regret.

Weeks later, Pete ran into Joyce, his high school sweetheart at Elvira's Market on Hillspoint Road. They had broken up over a silly argument, weeks before Pete met Simone. They ordered a pizza and sodas to go. They walked across the street to the beach, found an empty bench near the water's edge, and talked for hours.

Pizza and soda was followed by eggs and coffee the next morning in Joyce's kitchen. They professed their love for each other, and promised never to fight over trivial nonsense again. Five months later, Pete and

Joyce were married. A year later, Joyce gave birth to twin boys. Two years later, she gave birth to twin girls. Pete's dream of getting married and having a big family had finally come true.

Simone reflected on how quickly Pete's life had changed. She didn't know if Joyce was aware of their former relationship, but she didn't show disapproval whenever Simone called for Pete's help with her "honey-do" list. He found a partner to walk his desired path, and Simone was thrilled it was Joyce walking it with him, and not her.

* * * * * * *

Simone's first stop was the Verizon store. "Hi. I received this text a few months ago, and I'd like to know who sent it. She handed the phone to the clerk, who read the message:

I miss you, Simone. Your one and only true love, Joe.

He returned in a few minutes, along with his manager. "The text was sent from a burner phone so it couldn't be traced." The manager, who looked young enough to be in middle school, noticed Simone's disappointment.

"Do you think someone sent this to you as a joke?" he asked.

"No," she replied.

"Did you recently breakup with someone named Joe?" the manager inquired.

"Joe was my husband," Simone answered. "He was killed several years ago." Tears began filming her eyes. She dropped the phone into her purse. "Thanks," Simone said, and headed towards the door.

"If someone is harassing you, Miss, the police might be able to help," the manager said, his words trailing off as the door closed behind her.

She left Verizon, angry that someone was playing this sick joke. Why would someone torture her with such a message? She wiped her tears, and headed to her next stop, Victoria's Secret, in downtown Fairfield. Here, Simone spent fifteen minutes and purchased forty-five assorted underpants; lacey thongs, boy-shorts, yoga panties, and briefs. Simone agreed with Victoria Secret's motto:

There's no such thing as too many panties.

Her final stop, the local drop-off laundry, where she deposited her Victoria's Secret purchase, and asked if they could be ready for pick up by mid-afternoon.

"No problem," the clerk said without reacting, as if dropping off dozens of panties with price tags still attached, was a normal daily occurrence. "No problem, Miss, I'll remove tags."

Simone arrived at the office to find a phone message on her desk: Call Chief Jacobs. Jennifer Keys, Simone's business partner, took the message, raising her curiosity.

Jacobs said, "The neighbors have nothing to report. We will interview your housekeeper later this evening. I would suggest you change your locks, and keep your windows closed when you're not home."

Simone hung up the phone and mumbled to herself, "Great. I live in Westport, one of the most affluent towns on the gold coast of Connecticut, and now I have to be restrained in my own home."

"What's going on, Simone?" Jennifer asked, her hazel eyes squinting with curiosity, and snapping Simone out of her self-pity.

She hesitated a moment, and motioned for Jennifer to close her office door. "Well, I'm not supposed to discuss this with anyone, but I'm a bit freaked out. When I was getting dressed this morning, I discovered all my underwear missing. Every last pair of panties. Even the ones in my hamper."

"Ewww," responded Jennifer. "Who would steal your underwear?"

"I have no idea. Since they were in my dresser drawer and hamper before we left for Seattle, and you were with me the entire time, you're not a suspect."

"Gee, thanks . . . I think," Jennifer quipped. Lowering her voice she asked, "Not that it's any of my business, but what did you do about your problem this morning? I mean, did you have any underwear left? Unless you're not wearing any."

Simone laughed. "You know I'm a practical woman, Jen. I have a box in my closet of throw away clothes. Whenever I travel to a place I've never been to before, and plan to bring back souvenirs, I pack my ratty old clothes . . . socks with holes . . . panties with worn elastic . . . old pajamas. At the end of the day, I throw away the old clothes, and voilà, room for souvenirs."

"I learn something new about you every day, Simone." Jennifer said. "I had no idea you were so pragmatic."

"Just don't say anything to Katy and Jonathan."

"That you're not wearing panties?" she joked, trying to lighten Simone's mood.

Simone chuckled. "No, about the underwear being stolen. It gives me the creeps talking about it. Until this gets figured out, everyone is a suspect. Now I have to find a locksmith to change the lock on my front door. Let's catch up later."

Jennifer left, closing Simone's office door behind her.

Simon's first go-to person was, of course, Pete. She dialed his number, but got a recording saying he was out of town for a week. Simone left a message about her lock, but also said it wasn't important.

She then scrolled through her cell phone for a local locksmith. She called, and arranged an appointment within the hour.

The second phone message was from a potential client. She asked Jennifer to come back into her office, handing her the pink phone message slip.

"Jennifer, please call Barbara Kemp. She seems to be shopping for a wedding planner. I've had several conversations with her, and she'd fit our clientele. I think we need to be aggressive with her; offer her something other planners can't. Suggest a meeting at her place in New York City early next week."

Jennifer closed the office door and sat in a chair across from Simone. She lowered her voice and suggested, "How about we bring Jonathan with us? Kemp struck up a rapport with him when she came into the office unannounced last week. She said she was shopping in Westport, but I think she wanted to see what our offices looked like. Besides, there's nothing wrong with bringing eye candy with us," Jennifer added.

Simone stalled for a few moments to think about Jennifer's suggestion. "I think you're on to something, Jen. From what Jonathan told me, they did seem to hit it off, and eye candy could never hurt our prospects. That's a great idea. Call her back, set up a meeting, and text me an update. Meanwhile, I have to go back to my house and wait for a locksmith."

On her drive home, she thought about her staff. Could any one of them be the culprit?

Katy Lewiston and Jonathan Vasquez, have been working for Simone since she purchased the business a few years ago. They also worked for the previous owner for several years.

Katy was an attractive woman in her early forties, lived in Weston with her husband and sixteen year old son, Ryan. Katy liked working sweet-sixteen parties, bridal, and baby showers, and had a pulse on the latest décor and fashions. She could be impulsive at times, and a bit giddy, but she was a solid worker who took her job seriously.

Simone's mind wandered to Katy's son. Could he also be a suspect? But how would Katy, or her son, get a key to Simone's house? She dismissed the thought.

The same preoccupation applied to Jonathan: how would he get a key? Jonathan was thirty-four, 6'3", trim, and had dreamy-looking brown eyes. Jonathan worked well with anxious grooms, blended families, or same-sex marriages. He was equally comfortable working Bat and Bar Mitzvahs. The women referred to him as eye candy because they watched brides (and some grooms) checking out his good looks and attractive physique.

Jonathan never discussed his private life, and Simone preferred it that way. She had a rule about that, and wanted her employees to follow suit. Simone dealt with enough drama from brides, she didn't need it from her employees, too. Only Jennifer got a glimpse of Simone's private life, but not often.

It wasn't possible for either one of them to have access to her house key. She had never given them one, and didn't keep a key in the office.

Simone's phone suddenly pinged with an incoming text. At the next traffic light, she lifted her phone from her purse and read the message:

Don't ever leave me again. Joe

Two

Jack the locksmith was a balding man, late 50s, and seventy-five pounds overweight. Simone, at 5'1" was taller than him. He arrived in a mud-splattered, white panel truck, the dashboard, seen through a cracked windshield was cluttered with papers, crumpled McDonald's bags and empty coffee cups. The driver's door had peeling black lettering that read: *Call Jacques to Change Your Locks.* Tacky, thought Simone.

His yellowing tee shirt barely covered his stomach, and never crossed paths with bleach. His jeans were held up by a leather belt, tied low under his abdomen, emphasizing his enormous gut. When he bent over to inspect the latch, Simone got a full view of his butt crack. She wanted to mimic Jennifer, and say, 'Ewww.' Instead, she walked away, wishing she could burn her eyes to remove the image.

"Remember, Miss, don't give your key out to just anybody. There's a lot of nuts out there," he advised.

"I'm aware of that."

"Did you have a robbery? Was anything stolen? Were you home? Were you assaulted? You're a very attractive woman," he said giving her a once over. "Even though this is Westport, there are still assaults and robberies. A woman was recently raped, not far from here. You should think about getting a guard dog. You want me to install a dead bolt? Keeps you safe while you're sleeping."

"No, just the new lock is fine." Simone wanted him out of her house. He was making her uncomfortable, listening to his stories about assaults and rapes, and asking too many questions. Her gut instincts were telling her to be cautious. She assumed this was the quality of workman available when you needed an emergency locksmith.

"Here's your bill, Miss. I have to go back to my truck to make copies of the key. How many do you want? If you'd like, I can keep a copy in my shop, in case you get locked out."

"No," she responded quickly. "That's not necessary. I'd like to have all the keys. Four copies is fine."

He returned a short time later with keys in hand. As Simone wrote the check, Jack's eyes took in her finely decorated home. "You know, I think I installed the original locks in this house years ago. Doesn't look the same . . ." His words were cut off as Simone thrust the check in his hand, and quickly opened the front door for him to leave.

"Thank you for coming on such short notice," she said. He attempted to engage in additional small talk, but Simone said she had calls to make, and abruptly ended the conversation.

She felt a sudden wave of relief when she locked the door after him, but she still felt vulnerable. She watched him drive away. Maybe he was trying to give her good advice, and she took it the wrong way. And yet, something about him just didn't sit right with her. She thought of his parting advice about a dog.

"Yeah, I'll get a guard dog – to bite you if you ever show up here again," she said out loud to no one but herself.

Three

Simone, Jennifer and Jonathan rode Metro North to Grand Central Station. Two subways, and a brisk walk later, they arrived at Barbara Kemp and Biff Bradshaw's luxurious apartment on Central Park West. Simone was grateful no one suggested hailing a taxi from the 42nd Street terminal. Years ago, during an icy rain storm in New York City, Simone and her husband, Joe, were hit by a speeding taxi. He was killed, and she was seriously injured and sustained a miscarriage. Today, she was glad to have Jennifer and Jonathan with her, to keep her distracted from the memories and fears that haunted her every time she stepped off a curb.

Barbara and Biff's well-appointed apartment resembled sales catalogues for Henredon Furniture, Boca do Lobo and Crate and Barrel. After brief introductions, accolades on the décor and the view of Central Park poured forth.

Barbara was dressed in a sapphire blue Versace outfit that matched her eyes. She stood at least a foot taller than Simone, giving her a towering, commanding appearance. Jennifer, in her 6" Ferragamo's stood equally as tall. Both ladies must have read the handbook, *"How-to-Walk-NYC-in High Heels,"* something Simone would never consider doing.

Biff wore tan slacks, wing-tipped shoes, and a blue Ralph Lauren shirt, his muscles straining against the material. He stood an inch taller than Barbara, and when side by side, smiling simultaneously, they resembled Barbie and Ken.

The Kemp family came to America in the early 1800s, making their fortune in railroads. Descendants dated back to the middle ages in England, but it was the New World that promised them wealth in growing industries.

The Bradshaw family also came from England in the early 1800s. Biff's great grandfather worked for the Woolworth Brothers, and made his fortune in the five-and-dime business.

Barbara and Biff met at Stanford, dated during their four years, and planned to be married in Paris within the year. Both families approved, and encouraged this money-marrying-money marriage.

"Barbara and Biff," Simone started, "Is there anything you 'must have'? For example, must the wedding be in Paris, or, must you wear a certain designer's gown?"

Biff answered first. My parents got married at Notre Dame, and ever since I was little, they hoped I would get married there as well. Sounds corny, I know."

Simone recalled her reaction when she first visited Notre Dame, and a year later, the romantic honeymoon she and Joe shared in Paris. Her voice caught in her throat, but she continued.

"Not corny at all. It is a very romantic church in one of the world's most-beautiful cities." Turning to Barbara, she asked, "Can you think of any 'must-haves'?"

"Well, I can think of a few, which you might think trivial. First, I must have my father walk me down the aisle. And, I must have a full length Vera Wang gown with a long train. And, I must marry Biff." She completed her list by giving Biff an affectionate kiss on the cheek, accompanied by a big smile. Simone noticed that Barbara's mouth, full of blinding white teeth, hardly moved when she spoke. Her small, turned-up nose wiggled a little, like Samantha's on Bewitched.

"If you agree, we can research the terms and conditions for having the wedding in Notre Dame, with a reception at a local restaurant. How do your parents feel about a destination wedding? Do you think your guests will attend, being it will be a large travel expense for them?"

Barbara replied, her fingers entwined in Biff's, "My parents have a large home . . . more of a compound . . . outside of Paris that can house the immediate family. The other guests can stay in hotels, which they can easily afford." Simone thought this was a bit presumptuous of Barbara, but she knew her relatives and friends.

"We are planning an intimate wedding, with no more than one hundred twenty-five people."

"And what is your budget?" Simone asked directly.

"$225,000" answered Barbara. "And not a penny more," she added.

It was a comfortable budget, given the wedding was in Paris. "We will do our best to keep within the limits," Simone replied, not showing a reaction. Many of the weddings contracted at "I Do" LLC fall into that budgetary amount. In fact, at $225,000, the budget might be tight, if Barbara and Biff's honeymoon plans of traveling for six months was included in that amount.

Barbara continued, "My parents speak fluent French; I can get by. We need someone who speaks French, understands the culture, and can do the research for us. My parents are very busy with the family business, and neither Biff nor I have full command of the language. Do you have a staff member who can handle those requirements?"

Before Simone could answer, Jonathan chimed in, "Simone's your gal," giving Barbara a warm smile. Simone noticed he had a twinkle in his eyes, which she found mesmerizing. "She speaks fluent French," he added.

"Yes, I do," Simone said, reinforcing Jonathan's announcement. "My father was born in France, and we only spoke French at home. I tutored as well."

"You're hired," Biff and Barbara said in unison. Simone gave Jonathan a 'good job' look of encouragement. He smiled back, his smile reaching his twinkling eyes.

Jennifer took notes while Simone asked the standard questions about their desired wedding date, décor and food. Biff seemed more interested in showing Jonathan his sports memorabilia collection than discussing the wedding. "I'd prefer to stay out of the hen house, if you know what I mean." Jonathan nodded in agreement.

Biff poured a generous glass of bourbon, then offered Jonathan a cocktail. "Thanks, but the boss doesn't like us to drink on the job."

"Hen house," sniped Biff. The two men laughed. Biff took a large swig from his glass, and whispered, "Hey, ever tap that piece of ass?" referring to Simone.

Jonathan was thunderstruck by the crude question. He watched as Bradshaw poured another equally substantial glass of bourbon, and answered, "No." Jonathan turned and looked at Simone and Jennifer with empathy, wondering how many times they've been hit on by clients. He felt a brotherly affection towards the women; as if he needed to protect them from this predator.

"Too bad," said Bradshaw as he gave Jonathan a firm slap on the back.

Changing the subject, and wanting to get away from Biff, Jonathan asked, "May I use your rest room?"

"Sure. There's one in the master bedroom. Down the hall, on the left. Don't go in the powder room, the tiles were set this morning and the grout is drying."

As he headed towards the bedroom, Jonathan heard the clink of the crystal stopper being removed from the decanter, and then the distinct sound of ice cubes being dropped into a crystal glass. *It's only noon, and he's on this third drink,* thought Jonathan.

When he returned, Biff and Barbara were signing the wedding contract with Simone.

Handshakes, smiles, and promises of updates were exchanged. Biff held Simone's hand longer than Jonathan felt appropriate.

The three left the apartment, elated. As they headed towards the subway Simone said, "That was one of the easiest contracts I've ever procured. Thank you, Jonathan for developing the relationship while Jen and I were away. You did a great job. In fact, Jennifer and I would like you to be the point person in the wedding plans."

"Wow, this is a big surprise," he said excitedly. It was an opportunity to protect Simone from the hound, Biff. "Does this mean I'll go to Paris with you?"

"Yes. Since it is a contained wedding – no banquet hall and only one hundred twenty-five guests, Jennifer will stay behind. You've got a good head on your shoulders, and you know how to talk to the clients."

Jennifer suddenly stopped walking, folded her arms defensively, and asked Simone indignantly, "I'm not going to Paris?"

Simone wasn't sure if Jennifer was joking, or truly upset.

"I was looking forward to going to France – I've never been," she continued.

"We will see how things evolve. The wedding is months away, and a lot can happen before then. Jen, if you're willing to pay your own way, you can come to Paris with us. Since Barbara and Biff like Jonathan, it makes sense for him to come with me."

Simone didn't say she was thinking of inviting Charlie to come as well. After the wedding, they would go to Nice for a week's vacation. She was excited about going back to the City of Lights, albeit without Joe. But this time, with another man who owned her heart.

Charles Hamilton VI was the General Manager at the Grand Hamilton Hotel in Greenwich, Connecticut. Simone and Charlie had been involved in a passionate romance for almost two years. It started out as a one-night fling, which grew into a romantic whirlwind relationship. Charlie was in the midst of a divorce from a woman who wasn't ready to let go of her connection to the Hamilton money.

The three planners arrived back in Fairfield at six o'clock, too late for Simone to make calls to Paris. She would get on it early in the morning. Once she was back in her home, she slipped off her shoes and poured herself a glass of Pinot Gigio. She sat on her deck and reflected on what her father had once said, *One day you'll be happy you speak French, and you'll thank us for it.*

Now, her knowledge of the language had gotten her a signed contract, and a trip back to her favorite city. Though she hated to admit it, her father had been right. She closed her eyes and enjoyed the lasting rays of the sunset.

Four

The following morning, Simone noticed her car's front driver's side tire was low. This was the third time in two weeks it had needed air. She couldn't ignore this any longer; she needed to bring the car to the Porsche dealer and have the tire checked.

She drove directly to the office. Calls to Paris this morning were her top priority, before the whole country shut down for lunch.

Upon arrival, Simone announced to Katy and Jonathan, "Jennifer and I need to make calls to Paris. My tire is low, and I need my car to be brought to the dealer on Commerce Drive. Can one of you help me out?"

They both said, "Yes" simultaneously.

Jonathan turned to Katy and said, "If the tire goes flat while you're driving to the dealer, do you know how to change it?"

"All I know how to do is call AAA, my husband, or stick my thumb out," Katy said, poking fun at herself. She paused. "You win, Jonathan. You take the car."

Simone tossed the keys to him. "Be careful with my baby."

"Simone, would you mind if I stopped at Home Depot on my way back? It's not far from the dealer. I'd like to buy a bulletin board for my desk wall."

"Sure. But don't do the 'guy thing' and wander around the store for hours with glazed eyes."

Jennifer walked into Simone's office and closed the door. "Simone, before you call Paris, there's something we need to discuss."

Simone put down her cell phone, certain that Jennifer was going to complain about not going to Paris. "Is anything wrong?" Simone asked.

"I've got a problem. I received a call from my mother last evening. My father is in St. Francis Hospital. He's dying. I need to take time off to be with my family."

Simone knew Jennifer's father was ill, but didn't realize it was so serious. "I'm sorry to hear that."

"I think his drinking finally caught up with him. When I saw him a few months ago, his eyes were yellow. My mother said his liver is gone. But that didn't stop him. I guess the pain lessens when your body is pickled with whiskey."

"Would you like company?" Simone asked. "While you're with your family, it'll give me the opportunity to catch up with a college friend who lives in Sag Harbor."

"That would be great," Jennifer answered. "I need to leave later this afternoon, if that's okay with you."

Simone said, "I need to place calls to Paris. Once Jonathan is back, we can go." Simone called Notre Dame de Paris, while Jennifer sat in a chair near her partner, poised to take notes.

"I hope they speak English," quipped Jennifer, "because I don't know how to take notes in French."

Simone chuckled. "Even if they do speak English, you'll have a problem understanding their accent. I'll repeat the information in English."

They were pleased to learn weddings were performed in Notre Dame for non-parishioners. The church offered complete wedding packages, including upgrades for a translator (which Simone could do), champagne toasts (real champagne and not the swill often served in the States), elopement packages, and transportation. The date Barbara and Biff wanted in September 2018, was available. Simone felt confident, and gave the administrator her business credit card number.

"Merci beaucoup," Simone said.

Jonathan returned a short while later with a bulletin board, hooks, and a hammer ready to decorate his office space.

"Your car is fixed," he announced. "Sorry I took so long. I had to wait while they put it on the lift; they found a small nail. No charge for the repair. That's a great car, Simone. I haven't driven your car since I picked up the invitations for the White's wedding. I had forgotten how much fun it is to drive."

"Don't get too used to it," Simone joked.

Simone watched as Jonathan hung the bulletin board. He tacked a photo of himself with a young boy sitting on his lap. She realized, she knew nothing about his personal life. Was she uncaring for not wanting to know more about her employees?

"Who's the child?" she asked. "He's adorable."

Jonathan hesitated. After a moment he said, "He's my sister's kid. She's pregnant with her second, so I babysit my nephew whenever she has a doctor's appointment, or is tired. She's due any day."

Simone wanted to ask where they lived, if there was a dad in the child's life, or if Jonathan lived with them. But she decided not to overstep the boundary.

Jennifer transposed her notes, adding them to Dropbox for the Kemp/Bradshaw Wedding.

"Jonathan, please read through the file, call Barbara Kemp, and give her an update," Simone requested. "We need to get menu ideas . . . foods they like, don't like, allergies, and if they're okay with frogs' legs being on the menu. It's a popular French dish. Ask her to send us a bank check for $100,000, to hold the church, and as a retainer for our services. The check needs to be here within three business days. Otherwise, we'll cancel the church," Simone added. "Also, Jennifer and I are heading for Long Island to visit Jennifer's family. Try to get to Barbara before we depart."

"I'll get right on it."

He pulled up the file from Dropbox, made a few notes on a pad, and called Ms. Kemp.

"Hi, Barbara. It's Jonathan. I wanted to relay some good news: Simone was able to secure the Notre Dame Cathedral for your desired date."

"That's terrific. I can't wait to tell Biff."

Jonathan's gut twisted when he heard his name. *I don't like the way he looks at Simone*, he wanted to say, but contained his thoughts. Before Barbara could gush over her fiancé any further, he continued, "Simone needs to know if there are any food restrictions, or if people would shriek if they saw frogs' legs on the menu."

Barbara chuckled. "We won't tell them. We'll say it's chicken."

Just to be cordial, Jonathan returned the laugh. He hated Biff, and wondered how he was going to work with them until the wedding. They discussed restaurants, color schemes, favors, décor, bridal party, and other pertinent information.

Barbara continued, "I can't believe this is really happening. Biff and I have talked about getting married in Paris for over three years, and it is coming true. Thank you, Jonathan. Please thank Simone and Jennifer, too."

"I will," Jonathan said. "I'll be in touch soon."

After the phone call, Jonathan called Simone with an update. "Barbara said she'll FedEx a check today; we should have it by ten tomorrow. Barbara said she'll include a list of foods they like, don't like, allergies, and food restrictions of their guests. She knows of two relatives who are gluten and dairy sensitive. Can you imagine being in France and not being able to eat cheese or bread?" Jonathan joked. "Barbara thinks we should tell the guests they're eating chicken instead of frogs' legs."

"I don't believe in lying to guests," replied Simone. "Especially when it comes to food. We have time, we can work around the menu. The important thing is securing the church and the reception venue."

"Great job, Jonathan," she said. She was pleased that he is taking this promotion seriously. She continued, "Be sure to put the updated information into the Dropbox file. If you have any questions, send me a text."

The next morning, right on time, Jonathan signed for the FedEx envelope containing the $100,000 check. Simone had left a deposit slip with him, requesting he deposit the funds while they were away.

When she returned from Long Island, Simone had planned to give Jonathan a $500 bonus for securing the client.

"Gee, Simone," he said when she gave him the check two weeks later. "I never expected this. This is most generous of you."

"You did a great job acquiring the Bradshaw Wedding, and I wanted to show my appreciation. Just don't spend it all at Home Depot," she teased.

"Absolutely not."

There was that twinkle again.

Five

The two women arrived at Jennifer's childhood home, exhausted and bleary eyed as a result of bumper to bumper traffic on the Long Island Expressway. While they stood outside the house, waiting for someone to answer the doorbell, Simone looked down and read the doormat, "Welcome to the Keogh Home."

"Who are the Keoghs?" Simone asked.

"We are. I am. I mean, that's my family's last name. Keys is my alias."

"Really? All the times I've spoken to your mother and called her Mrs. Keys, she never corrected me."

"She got used to it after a few years."

"What made you change your name?"

Jennifer hesitated to reply. She rang the bell again. After a brief silence, she answered Simone's question. "My father's name was frequently in the newspaper. He was arrested for drunk driving, disorderly conduct, and went to jail for beating a co-worker. He was fired from three jobs for showing up intoxicated."

Reflectively, she added, "I went to a Catholic elementary school until eighth grade. During that time, I was bullied unmercifully by my classmates, and sometimes, by the nuns. Once, when I was called to the principal's office, the nun said, 'If your father didn't spend all his money on Satan's poison, your parents wouldn't be behind in tuition payments.' People pointed and said, 'That's the Keogh kid.' I couldn't take the teasing and bullying any longer." Jennifer began to fish in her pocketbook for the key to her parent's home.

She continued, "When I graduated elementary school, I begged my parents to send me to the local public high school. That's when I decided to legally change my name. A fresh start, so to speak. I told my mother what I wanted to do. She cried for days, but she understood. Because I was a minor, she accompanied me to the attorney's office and signed the legal documents. She paid the lawyer out of the pin money she had squirreled away for years. That summer, I got a job at the local pizza parlor answering the phone, taking orders. Any money I got, I gave her. It took two years, but I paid her back every penny. Most of the students at the public school didn't know me, so as long as I kept my given name a secret, I avoided the bullying. There doesn't seem to be anyone home," Jennifer announced abruptly, concluding her story.

As Jennifer continued to rummage through her oversized pocketbook for the house keys, Simone looked at the surrounding homes. They were all the same, small, well-kept Cape Cod, or raised ranch styles with a car or two parked in the driveway. Simone assumed because the cars were parked outside, the garages had been renovated to become game rooms, dens, or a man cave. Or simply, another room to store excessive clutter.

Jennifer found the keys, opened the door, and turned on the lights in the darkened home. Inside, on the kitchen table, they found a note from her brother:

> *Jennifer, Dad is on life-support. He doesn't have long to live.*
> *Come to St. Francis immediately. T.*

"He couldn't text me," Jennifer said exasperated. "He's so inconsiderate."

Terrance, like his father, was an alcoholic. His father's love was whiskey, while Terrance's was vodka. The two men spent many nights sitting in the same bar, on the same stools, drinking the same booze. Meanwhile, Jennifer's mother, Bridgette, stayed home, making excuses for the men's absence and drinking.

Her father was now jaundice and dying of hepatitis and cirrhosis of the liver. He had tubes coming out of practically every orifice. Simone stayed in the waiting room, remembering her parents, and how she wished she could see them one more time. Jennifer joined her mother and brother in the curtained-off area of the ICU. She put her arm around her mother for support. Tears streamed down their faces as they listened to the beeps and hums from the life-support machines.

"We were waiting for you to get here, so you could say goodbye to your father," her mother said through her tears. "Your brother and I have instructed the doctors to take him off life-support."

Forty-five minutes later, Patrick Terrance Keogh died. Simone gave Bridgette a hug and expressed her sympathies. "I'm sorry, Mrs. Keogh."

Bridgette smiled at Simone upon hearing her married name. Simone wondered why Jennifer had never told her that her last name was Keogh. "If there is anything I can do to help, please let me know," she offered the older woman.

"Thank you, Simone. Your being here means the world to me."

Bridgette took Simone's arm and pulled her aside, away from the others. With the trace of an Irish accent, Bridgette whispered, "Please Simone, watch over Jennifer. I worry about her. She can't seem to find a good man to marry. She needs someone who can put up with her wild ways. I was married, and had two small children by the time I was twenty-two. She needs to stop spending all her money on clothes. And those shoes! She needs to be careful. She goes around with bad men – she married two of them. *Go n-ithe an cat thú is go n-ithe an diabhal an cat,*" she said in Gaelic, as she made the Sign of the Cross.

"What does that mean, Mrs. Keogh?" asked Simone.

"It loses its meaning in translation," said the elderly woman, wiping away fresh tears. "It means, if a cat gobbled up its enemy, like a can of tuna, that the devil should eat them both. Jennifer is like a cat running after these bad men. One day, the devil will get them both."

Simone wanted to say that she didn't interfere in Jennifer's private life, but she held back. She reflected on how Jennifer was attracted to Robert Hathaway, the skanky security guard at the Hamilton Hotel. Simone could see why Jennifer's mother was concerned, and wondered what Jennifer's two husbands were like.

"I'll do my best," she promised.

The funeral was two days later. It was a one-day wake with the burial the following morning. Surprisingly, it was not a typical Irish funeral: no drinking, no bagpipes, and no Mass, only a simple prayer at the funeral home, and again at the cemetery. Simone stayed by Jennifer's side, but slipped into the background whenever family and friends approached to pay their respects.

Simone thought back on her parents' funeral. They were killed in an automobile accident, the result of her father's drinking. She was estranged from her father after she left Kentucky to pursue her college education at NYU. He, too, was an alcoholic who abused her, and her mother. Similarly, Jennifer had a dysfunctional relationship with her father. While their childhoods were different, so much was the same.

"You probably need to get back to the office, Simone, I'll take the Long Island Railroad back. I want to help my mother go through my dad's clothes and paperwork. My brother is useless, he's already drunk. I'll be here for a few more days."

"I'm here for you, Jennifer, and will stay as long as you need me. The clients will still be there when we return. Besides, Katy updated me, and everything is running smoothly."

On the drive to the Keogh home, Simone revisited the subject of Jennifer's alias. "You know Jennifer, we have much more in common than you think." She proceeded to tell Jennifer her backstory. "My birth name is Alison-Simone Deschamps. I hated having a double first name, which my father insisted I use. Alison was his mother's name. Simone was my maternal grandmother's name."

She continued, "Once, a classmate called our home and asked for Ali. My father answered, and told her there wasn't anyone there by that name. I grabbed the phone and told my friend I'd see her at school. My father threatened to send me to a boarding school where they would call me Alison-Simone. "When I applied for college, I used only Simone. And Simpson was Joe's last name."

"Simone, you're like an onion. Every time you peel away another layer, I learn new things about you. I knew Simpson was Joe's last name, but I had no idea about your given name. Thanks for sharing. It helps to know that I'm not alone."

Simone and Jennifer returned to Connecticut four days later. She drove Jennifer to her Fairfield apartment. "Do you want me to stay with you?"

"Thanks, Simone. But there's nothing else I can do, or say. I feel sorry for my mother. She will now have to care for my brother, another alcoholic. I'm fine. I'll see you in the office tomorrow. I just need to get a good night's sleep. Thanks again for coming to the Island with me."

Simone headed back to her house in Westport. It was after eleven at night and the Post Road was empty of cars and pedestrians, so the ride home took less than fifteen minutes. As she drove, she thought, *yes, a good night's sleep would do wonders.* During her time in Long Island, she stayed at a local B&B with a lumpy bed, bad lighting, and rubbery-tasting breakfast muffins. Jennifer stayed with her mother, and slept in her old bedroom. Simone recalled the nights she spent wandering around the house she grew up in when she returned to Louisville for her parent's funeral. Those memories stirred up nightmares she'd rather forget.

Simone stopped her car in front of her house, and pressed the garage door opener. While waiting for the door to ascend, she looked at her unwelcoming-looking home. She decided she'd need to do something about installing motion lights or plug-in timers. She thought to herself, *maybe I'll get a guard dog, as Jack had suggested.* Simone laughed at the thought of Jack the locksmith, and his protruding gut and exposed butt crack.

She walked up the flight of stairs from the garage that led to her living room, and entered the darkened house. The ambient light from the street lamps guided her through the rooms. She opened the French doors in her living room, which released a stale, but sweet smell that permeated the house. She assumed it came from rotting fruit she had carelessly left on her kitchen counter. She would take care of it in the morning.

She walked into her bathroom, brushed her teeth, and washed her face. In her bedroom, she stripped out of her wrinkled clothes, got under the welcoming covers, and was sound asleep in minutes.

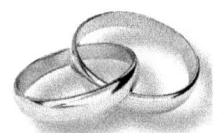

Six

Simone awoke to her six-thirty alarm. She showered, dressed, and rummaged through her suitcase for her makeup. Then, she decided to put away the items tossed from the suitcase: dirty laundry, shoes and a few outfits. She didn't want to return home later to disorganized clutter.

She hoped to get to the office by eight. Her watch read seven twenty-five. No time to make breakfast, but enough time for a cup of much-needed coffee for her travel mug. She would stop at McDonald's drive-through and also get an Egg McMuffin.

She walked toward her kitchen. The sweet, citrus smell became stronger with every step. Then, she froze, her eyes fixed on her granite counter. In her oversized, cut-crystal vase stood dozens of long stemmed red roses, emitting their fragrance. Her mind flash-backed to the romantic evening, years ago in Joe's Manhattan apartment, when he proposed marriage. Dozens of roses were arranged all around his apartment for the occasion.

"What the hell," she said out loud.

She looked for a card, but there was none. No telltale signs of where the flowers were purchased, handwriting to analyze, or who had delivered them. She opened her kitchen utility drawer, and retrieved the business card.

"Hello, Chief Jacobs? It happened again."

Within fifteen minutes, two police cars were outside Simone's home on Compo Road.

"When did you discover the flowers?" the Chief asked.

"Right before I called you. I got home late last night after being away for a few days. I went directly to sleep. I did smell a sweet scent, but I thought it must have been fruit I left on the kitchen counter."

"Did you leave these French doors open all night?" the Chief asked, a bit of reprimand in her voice. "And, did you change the locks after the last incident?" Jacobs inquired.

"Yes, I did change the lock on the front door," avoiding the Chief's question about the French doors. "Now that you've mentioned it, the guy who came to change the lock . . . Jack . . . Jacques . . . was creepy. He offered to keep a copy of my key in his office, in case I got locked out, but I declined. He went to his truck and made copies. Maybe he made an extra one, and used it." Simone was getting a sick feeling in her stomach, thinking of Jack prowling inside her house when she wasn't there.

"We'll check him out," said one of the officers.

"Meanwhile, I hate to say it, you'll need to change your locks again," the Chief said sympathetically. Trying to lighten Simone's burden, she said, "As for the flowers, you could throw them out, or drop them off at the local senior center."

Simone could only give out a moan. Or, was that her stomach growling? And why did the Chief keep saying, "locks" when she only had one lock on her door? She dismissed the question.

She secured her windows and French doors, making sure her front door was locked. "This is so annoying," she mumbled to herself. She walked down the flight of stairs to the garage, shoved the bunch of roses into the trash can, got in her car and drove off. Thoughts of an Egg McMuffin were equally tossed.

Seven

Pushing back the memory of the flowers, Simone arrived at her office frustrated and grumpy. She prepared an Espresso, grabbed several Munchkins Katy had generously brought to the office, and headed to her desk. After a few minutes, she felt rejuvenated from the caffeine and sugar high.

She stood at the threshold of her office and said, "Jonathan, I have a Home Depot errand for you."

"Yes?" he asked excitedly as he jumped up from his chair. "What do you need – a table saw . . . a power drill . . . a lawn mower?"

Simone chuckled. "No, not any of those. You're funny. I need a lock for a front door. Just the tumbler. And ask the locksmith to make three copies of the master key. Mine broke in the lock this morning," she fibbed. "Thank you for doing this. I have to make calls to Paris. Apparently, Miss Kemp wants all the extras offered by the Church. Jennifer and I have to find a restaurant that will accommodate everyone, including serving gluten and dairy free food. I hope the maître d' doesn't hang up on me."

After Jonathan left, she called Jennifer into her office, and closed the door behind her. Simone often felt she was in a fishbowl, as the walls and the door were three-quarters glass. It was a 'clean' look Simone liked, but it also made her feel vulnerable. She abhorred office walls covered with random photos, papers and cartoons. In her office, she could have a private meeting, while knowing what was going on outside her door.

"Jen, you're not going to believe this. I found dozens of roses – possibly fifty - in my kitchen this morning."

"Really? Maybe Charlie left them for you."

"Charlie doesn't have a key to my house." This made Jennifer raise an eyebrow, but she knew better than to ask Simone 'why not'. "I doubt it was Charlie. Although, I'm going to have to discretely ask him."

"I heard you say you broke your key in the lock."

"Yes, the Police Chief still thinks I shouldn't mention this to anyone. I haven't even told Charlie what's going on. If he had left the flowers, I'm sure he would have left a card. ARGH! I don't have time for this. After I finish talking to Charlie, we need to call Paris."

"Tap on the glass when you're ready. I'll wear my beret to get into the mood."

Jennifer always knew how to break the tension with a snarky remark, a joke, or light humor. Just as Jennifer was about to leave, Simone asked her, "Jennifer, I know you are upset you're not going to Paris, but I don't think it's fair to charge a client for an additional planner."

Jennifer thought for a moment. "It's the correct decision. Although, I was dreaming of all the latest designer shoes I could purchase," she said through a laugh. "If I decide to go, I'll pay my own way. I have no problem with that. Let's see how busy we are at the time of the Bradshaw wedding. We can't leave Katy and the temps here alone in case a last minute event gets booked."

Simone thought for a moment. "Maybe we can ask Leslie, who interned with us last year, to help out in case a client calls."

"Whatever happened to her?" asked Jennifer.

"She got a job with a large New York event company. We keep in touch by e-mails, holiday cards and an occasional phone call. Before I say anything to her, let's see how this wedding comes together."

"A good point," said Jennifer.

"I've been thinking, Jennifer, that after Paris you and I should create a strategic plan for hiring additional staff. Our profits have steadily increased over the past two years. Maybe consider moving Jonathan and Katy up to full time planners. We also need to hire a Social Media specialist who can do the work Katy's son is doing. He's going off to college soon, and we should have an in-house, full time web person."

Simone paused. "I have an idea. Let's do an overnight at the Norwich Spa. We can get massages, facials and attend a candlelight yoga class.

We'll reserve a conference room, and hire a strategic planner to help us with our business plan."

"Simone, that's a wonderful idea," Jennifer replied enthusiastically, her eyes wide with excitement. "We both need time away." Jennifer looked at her watch. "Let's discuss this later. You need to call Charlie, and then Paris, before the vendors leave for the day."

Jennifer closed Simone's office door, and returned to her desk.

After pleasantries, Simone told Charlie about the flowers. "You won't believe what I found when I got home from the funeral. One of my clients left me a dozen roses, as a thank you for doing a great job with their daughter's Sweet Sixteen. Jennifer got a dozen too. Isn't that sweet?"

"That's very thoughtful. Gee, Simone, I have to remember that the next time you do something extra special for me," Charlie said, teasing.

Simone immediately knew he wasn't the one who had left the flowers. Disappointment filled her heart, while a sudden shiver of fear ran through her body.

"How about we meet at 6:00 at DaPietro's for dinner?" she asked.

"Perfect. I've missed you. I look forward to seeing you later. Love you, Simone," Charlie whispered into the phone.

"Me, too," she responded.

After Simone's husband died, she never thought she could love again. But, Charlie proved her wrong. Although he would like them to live together, she was hesitant about a deeper commitment. She liked it the way it was. He lived in Greenwich, she in Westport. Both worked long hours, and often, on weekends. She traveled frequently. He didn't. She enjoyed her independence and freedom, and didn't want their relationship to progress past this point. At least, not until Charlie's divorce was finalized, he completed his MBA, and he decided what he wanted to do with the rest of his life.

Charlie was considering leaving the family business. He worked eighty hours a week, and his efforts went unappreciated and unnoticed by his father. Eve, his soon-to-be ex-wife came to the hotel, flaunting her latest and newest lovers. His nephew, Frederick Murphy, was back on the grounds, even though Charlie had fired him for insubordination.

Charlie's father - Frederick's grandfather - overrode Charlie's authority and rehired Frederick. His nephew stayed out of his uncle's way, but every time Charlie saw Frederick, he felt a knot in the pit of his stomach.

Frederick had told Eve that he saw Charlie and Simone at the hotel having dinner together after a charity wedding. It was the first night that started their passion-filled affair, and the beginning of Eve's plot to destroy Charlie, and get her hands on the Hamilton money.

His nephew had planted listening devices in Charlie and Simone's rooms, as well as Casey Bouvier, a bride who was murdered on her wedding day. Frederick knew Casey when they both attended Princeton. He also told Mr. and Mrs. Bouvier, the bride's parents, that Charlie was partying with Simone during their daughter's memorial service yards away in the hotel. His irresponsible antics were embarrassing for Charlie, the hotel, the Bouvier family, and his father.

Frederick's goal was to usurp his uncle out of his position in the Hamilton Hotel, and eventually move into his chair. Power, and the ability to hire and fire people, fueled Frederick's ego. Except, it was these euphoric and immature actions that got him sacked.

Charlie was embarrassed when his father rehired Frederick. As a result, Charlie no longer enjoyed the office environment, and didn't see any future moving up to the hotel's corporate offices. Conversely, if he moved to a higher position, he'd be sitting only feet away from his father's disapproving stare. His thoughts were to leave the hotel after obtaining his MBA, look for a job at a corporate company, and maybe work nine-to-five, with weekends off.

Charlie's dream was to someday marry Simone, and start a family. He was thirty-seven years old, and time was marching forward. He wanted to move forward as well. Eve had lied to him for a decade, saying she was trying to get pregnant. But one day, while Charlie was rummaging through one of her bureau drawers looking for his watch, he found her birth control pills.

Simone loved Charlie, but didn't feel she could confide in him about the stolen underwear, the mysterious flowers, or the texts. Or, the fact that she had over $15 million in the bank, a combination of money from her parent's, Joe's estates and her successful business. Why, didn't she trust him? Did he have a dark side she didn't know about, and was he the one who stole her underwear and left the flowers? Although she had worked through her fear of losing Charlie, as she had lost Joe, she still kept a wall of distance. This, was unsettling. Right now, she had more important matters to figure out, like who was getting into her house, and who was the owner of her prized lingerie.

After speaking to Charlie, she called Pete, her reliable handyman, and asked if he could meet her at her house at five o'clock. He promptly showed up.

"The first time, I broke the key in the lock," she fibbed. "Then, today, I lost my keys," she fibbed again. "And so, here you are to the rescue," she said, trying to sound nonchalant. Simone wouldn't consider Pete a gossiper, but, since he did a lot of work in the area, she didn't want to take a chance he would repeat the story of the break-ins.

"Simone, I'm sorry I wasn't here to help you out the last time. Joyce and I went to Bermuda for our anniversary. I felt bad when I got back and heard your message." He changed the tumbler and handed over the four keys. "Just don't lose this set."

They stood outside her door on her cement stoop. "Pete, before you go . . . do you know Jack, the locksmith? He goes by Jacques. He seemed a little creepy to me." Simone had noticed Jack's truck in the area a few times since he changed the lock, making her feel he was stalking her. Most likely it was her imagination, and he was working in the area, but she didn't trust him.

"Jack . . . yeah, he's an okay guy . . . a little sloppy-looking, but harmless. He's been in business for years. Remember, Simone, I'm only a phone call away. If you need anything, any time of the day or night, call or text me."

"I will. Thanks, Pete," Simone said. They chatted about the kids, and he showed her photographs of the latest arrival.

"I'm so glad your dream of starting a family came true. Joyce is a wonderful woman. Happy Anniversary."

"Thanks Simone. I'll always treasure the time you and I had together. But Joyce," . . . his voice trailed off . . . "she loves being married to me, and being a mom."

They embraced, and gave each other a kiss on the cheek.
It was comforting knowing Pete. He was honest, and trustworthy.
Or, was he?

Eight

Simone's fatigue was mounting. She couldn't sleep, her mind obsessed about who was getting into her house. Every noise made her bolt up in bed. Her business was heading into its busy season, but the long hours and distractions weren't enough to keep her mind from wondering about the break-ins. Her days were filled with hiring office temps, interviewing social media specialists, web designers, and increasing her list of reliable and professional vendors. In addition, she had to deal with her personal life wrecked with invasions, lock changes, and mysterious texts. She needed a day to herself.

Every Thursday morning Simone facilitated an office meeting with her staff. They updated each other on active events planned for the next three weeks. They discussed pending contracts, recently completed events, and the 'wish list,' consisting of cold calls, call-in inquiries, and any proposals sent to prospective clients.

One of the active events was the upcoming Kemp/Bradshaw wedding. Simone started, "We'll be leaving for Paris in a few days. Notre Dame is all set, and the reception will be at Le Cinq restaurant in the Four Seasons Hotel on the Champs-Elysees. There will be one hundred and seventy-five guests; more than expected. The manager assured me they can accommodate the gluten and dairy-free folks, and their allergy restrictions. Barbara is allergic to soy, Biff to hazelnuts, and his cousin is allergic to snails. Fortunately, the Kemp's have agreed to increase their budget by $50,000."

Simone continued, "Barbara's gown is ready. She's picking it up tomorrow, and taking it with her in her carry-on bag. She is not willing to take the chance the dress will end up in Paris, New York rather than

Paris, France. The hotel referred them to a florist, photographer and a band. There are copies of all the contracts in the file, except the photographer. Jonathan, please e-mail him, the address is in the file. Remind him it is imperative he send us a copy of the signed contract. He understands English. Please print out a copy of all the e-mails, guest lists, seating plan, contracts, and any other pertinent information. Be sure all the papers are in my messenger bag, ready for transport. The couple bought wedding insurance, a smart decision given this is a destination wedding."

Simone turned and asked, "Jonathan, do you have anything to add?"

"Yes. I spoke to Biff. He said his groomsmen are renting their tuxedos in Paris, through Barbara's father, and he picked up the rings and will bring them to Paris. I checked with all of the vendors, and they have received their deposit checks. They've all signed the agreement to be paid in full at the conclusion of the wedding. They will accept your American Express Card, so no problem with money having to be exchanged into Euros."

He paused for a few seconds, obvious he had something more to say.

"Is there anything else?" Simone asked.

Jonathan hesitated, then continued, "His best man has organized a bachelor party at a Paris nightclub. Simone, Biff invited me. May I go?"

Simone looked at Jonathan and stalled for a few moments, considering this request. "Jonathan, these are your clients, not your friends. Sorry, but, no. Anything else?"

Jonathan shook his head, disappointedly. His request didn't sit well with Simone. She glanced over at Jennifer, who seemed indifferent. But, Jonathan was young, excited about his first trip to Paris, and, after all, he was a guy.

Simone continued. "Jonathan will return on Sunday. I'm staying on in Paris, followed by a ten-day vacation." She didn't add that Charlie was joining her. "Jennifer will be in charge."

"Oh how nice," Katy added. "Where are you staying after Paris?"

Simone wasn't going to share her personal life with the office staff, so she ignored Katy. She looked at her watch, and announced, "I'm meeting Marissa from the Fairfield Chamber of Commerce in a few minutes. After lunch, I'm going to IKEA. If you need me, send a text."

Simone packed up her messenger bag and headed off to her meeting with Marissa at Avellino's Restaurant. Her thoughts were interrupted by her cell phone. It was Marissa from the Chamber.

"I'm stuck in a meeting off site. I don't think I'll be back in time for lunch. Can we reschedule?"

"Absolutely," Simone tried not to respond with too much enthusiasm. "Not a problem. Send me an e-mail with some dates that work for you. Thanks Marissa."

Simone felt a weight being lifted. She decided to forgo IKEA, and instead, drove to the Porsche dealer. The oil warning light had come on when she started the car that morning. She hoped she hadn't pushed her luck, and did some damage to the engine. Lately, it seemed she never had time to take care of the little things, like her car, banking, or taking a day for herself. In hindsight, she should have had the oil changed when Jonathan brought the car in for the tire.

"Can you check to see why the oil light is on?" she asked Sal at the Porsche dealership.

"Sure, Simone." He checked his work log. "We're a little backed up this afternoon. If you leave the car, I'll give you a loaner if you bring it back by six o'clock." He handed a key to Simone. "It's the blue Macan, tag ending in 002. I think you'll enjoy driving it."

"Perfect. And thanks for taking care of my flat tire a couple of weeks ago."

Sal had a quizzical look on his face. "Tire? What was wrong with your tire?"

"I had a tire that kept losing air. One of my associates brought it in. He said you found a nail in the tire."

"Let me check the computer to be sure there wasn't a notation about you needing new tires." He typed in Simone's name. "No, I don't see it. The only thing I see is the last oil change." He looked up at Simone with a look of disapproval. "That was over eight months ago."

"I've been busy," she said, feeling like a schoolgirl being reprimanded for forgetting her homework.

He continued, "Quite often, a quick fix, like a low tire, or a blown fuse, doesn't get put into the system. It takes more time inputting the info into the computer, than fixing the problem. I'm sure whoever took care of your associate didn't think of inputting the information into the computer. Besides, a warning light would come on if there was a serious problem with the tire. Sometimes, it's just the car's computer . . . ."

He rambled on. Simone couldn't focus. His words were becoming jumbled. All she wanted to do was go home to take a nap. She picked up the car key from the counter and made her way to the door. "Thanks for the loaner, Sal. I'm late for an appointment. I'll be back before six."

She headed home, looking forward to playing hooky for the rest of the day. She pulled up in front of her house. Her hand automatically went to the visor to push the garage door opener, but she had left it in her car. And her house keys were on the key ring with the car keys. "Damn," she muttered. She dug in her oversized purse, found her small change pouch, and removed the extra house key she kept in there.

She found a parking space across the street, and parallel parked between two cars. She opened her gate, making a mental note to ask Pete to fix the squeak. Simone opened her front door and locked it behind her.

Like a zombie, she walked to her bedroom, stripped off her clothes, and put on a thick, comfy bathrobe. She washed her face, climbed into bed and was sound asleep in minutes.

She awoke an hour later feeling refreshed. Wow, a power nap really does work, she thought as she stretched and yawned. She considered what she'd like to do with the rest of the day, and decided she'd go for a walk on the beach, and then relax on her deck. She picked up her novel from the nightstand and thought, *Maybe I will finally finish this book.*

Suddenly, she heard the sound of the squeaking gate leading up to her house, followed by footsteps climbing the steps. She supposed it was a UPS or FedEx driver, dropping off a package. She froze in place when she heard the jingle of keys, and the sound of someone putting a key into the lock. Then, the doorknob turned and the front door was opened. She heard the click of the door being closed.

Her mind began to race . . . someone was inside her house . . . what was she to do? She grabbed her cell phone from the nightstand, then looked for a place to hide. She didn't hear anyone walking. The intruder had stopped. She stood still and listened. All she heard was her heart pounding in her chest.

There was a rustling sound, followed by a slap, followed by another slap. *Was the person putting on gloves?*

She then heard footsteps coming from the living room, then down the hallway, and toward her bedroom.

Her head turned right, then left, deciding where to run. Her closet, on the other side of the room, would force her to walk past the opened bedroom door. She would be seen. She dropped to the floor, and wiggled under her bed. She set her cell phone to 'silent' and dialed 911.

The prowler walked toward her bedroom. Simone held the cell phone against her chest, under her thick robe, muffling the sound of the operator, "911. What is your emergency?" She was afraid the burglar would hear the question, look under the bed, and find her. She disconnected the call.

She watched as a pair of blue paper booties walked around her bed. Booties, like those worn by a doctor in an operating room, or the police at a crime scene. She couldn't tell if it was a man or a woman. The intruder stopped at her nightstand, just a few inches from her face. She was certain her pounding heart could be heard over the rummaging near her nightstand.

Suddenly, the prowler's feet turned and the person exited the room. Shortly after, the front door closed. She wiggled out from under the bed, but the bathrobe's belt was stuck on the crossbar under the bed. "Damn," she muttered. She twisted and wriggled until she got the robe off her body. She scurried out from under the bed, leaving the bathrobe behind.

Running to her front door, she was about to swing it open, when she remembered she was completely naked. She ran back to her bedroom, retrieved her cell phone from under her bed, and called 911 again.

"Tell Chief Jacobs it happened again. And this time, I was home."

Nine

While Simone waited for the police to arrive, she dressed, and checked her room to see if anything was missing.

Chief Cindy Jacobs and two other police officers showed up within minutes.

"Ms. Simpson, are you okay?" Chief Jacobs asked. "We received a hang-up 911. It takes us longer to find the location from a cell than a land line. I'm glad you were able to call us back. Explain what happened."

"Whoever came into my house stood inches from my face," Simone said. "They wore paper blue booties, and I think, gloves, because I heard a slapping sound. The person rummaged through my nightstand, but I can't find anything missing. I heard them using a key, so I think it's someone who has a copy."

"At this point, Ms. Simpson, I'd suggest you get security cameras installed in your house. Apparently, changing the locks isn't helping. It could be a professional who knows how to pick a lock, so no matter what you do, they'll still get in."

While the officers were writing up their report, Simone told the Chief about the text messages. "I went to Verizon, and they said they were sent from a burner phone, and there wasn't anything they could do. It might be the same person who's coming into my house; I don't know."

"That would make the most sense," said the Chief. "Come to my office tomorrow, and we'll get the paperwork going for an investigation. I believe you've got a stalker on your hands. Have you received any threatening mail? Or, have you seen the same person in places where you've never seen them before?"

"As a matter of fact, I have. Jack, the locksmith."

"We checked him out the last time," said the Chief. "He has a monopoly on the new construction and renovations in the area, supplying new locks to the contractors. But, if you see him in the grocery store, or at the gym, or near your office, give me a call."

Simone left a few minutes later, and drove to the car dealer.

"It needed an oil change. Otherwise, it looks good," said Sal. "Are you okay, Simone? You look pale."

"I'm fine. It's been a long day. I've been traveling, and I think jet lag has caught up with me." She didn't want to have to explain her situation to another person.

She went through the motions and paid the bill. She retrieved her car and drove towards home in a daze, not believing what had happened two hours before. *Would they have killed me if they saw me,* she wondered? *Maybe it was time to tell Charlie what was going on.* They were leaving in a few days for the Bradshaw wedding, maybe she'd tell him then.

Simone's anxiety was rapidly escalating. She kept checking her rear view mirror to see if she was being followed. She turned down streets in the opposite direction to her home, just to see if another car was behind her. She pulled over to the curb, and waited for cars to pass, glancing at every driver to see if she recognized anyone. Paranoia was taking hold, a panic attack just breaths away from consuming her body. She pulled out of the space, made a U-turn, and drove straight to the office. She rushed in and looked for Jennifer, her eyes filled with fear, her hands shaking.

"What's happened, Simone, you look terrible," said Jonathan. He walked toward her, concerned.

Simone looked around, "Where's Jennifer?"

"She's in the conference room making phone calls. I'll get her," Jonathan said as he sprinted towards the back of the office.

Katy came from the kitchenette, and barraged Simone with questions: "What happened, Simone? Were you in a car accident? Are you okay? Do you want us to call the police?"

"Yes . . . no . . . I mean, I'm okay. I wasn't in a car accident. No, don't call the police. I just need to speak to Jennifer."

"Simone," Jennifer called from the back of the office. "Are you all right?"

Simone jogged toward her business partner, tears brimming. She grabbed Jennifer's arm and pulled her into the conference room. As soon as the door was closed, she broke down, sobbing.

"Someone came into my house while I was there. I hid under the bed. They were inches away from my face . . . the police came . . ."

"Did they take anything?"

"No," Simone shook her head. "That's the strange thing. They rummaged through my night stand, and left seconds later."

"Did you tell Jonathan and Katy what happened?"

"No. Remember, the Police Chief said not to tell anyone, because the intruder could be someone close to me. I think that's why I haven't yet told Charlie."

"Oh, Simone, you've got to tell him what's going on. He'll be furious if he finds out. What if the police interrogate him?"

"I never thought of that. Come to think of it, I don't know why they didn't question him the first time someone broke into my house. This is horrible."

Simone wiped her tears. She sat up straighter, looked at Jennifer and said, "There's more. Whoever this person is has also been sending me text messages, saying they're Joe. The police thinks I might have a stalker."

"Oh my God, Simone. When did that happen? Why didn't you tell me?"

"The first text came after we had lunch with Charlie's father following the Bouvier meeting. That was months ago, and I ignored it. A second one came about a week later. Then, they stopped. But they started up again after the first break-in. Verizon said they're being sent from a burner phone. Jen, I'm too scared to go home. I'm going to call Charlie and stay with him tonight. He's going to meet me in Paris, and then we're going to Nice for a week. I had planned to tell him then, but I now know, I can't wait until then."

Jennifer took the news about Charlie going to Paris with stride. Simone was so secretive about her life, that nothing surprised her any more.

"Jennifer, I think you should come to Paris with us. I hate to admit it, but I can't focus on this wedding. I feel out of touch with what needs to be done, and Jonathan isn't experienced enough to take on a destination wedding by himself. My problems should not be our client's problem; that's not fair to Biff and Barbara. We'll charge them for two planners, and we'll account your outlay as a company expense."

Now it was Jennifer's turn to pause for a moment before answering. "You know, Simone, going to Paris will be a huge sacrifice for me," she said sarcastically with a smirk on her face.

After a pause Simone smiled and said, "You always know how to cheer me up. Thank you."

"I'll go back to your house while you pack," offered Jennifer.

"While we're there, I'll call Anna Maria and ask her to thoroughly clean my house. It gives me the creeps knowing someone's been coming in and out."

Before they left the conference room, Simone hugged Jennifer. "Thank you for being my friend. I don't know what I would do without you."

"No matter what is going on in our lives, we know we have each other," Jennifer said.

The two women drove separately to Simone's house. Simone packed for an overnight stay, and called Anna Maria while Jennifer stood guard.

"Thanks, Jen. I appreciate you helping me out."

Trying to reassure Simone, she said, "I'm sure the police will have this figured out in no time. It might be a secret admirer who doesn't understand that such behavior is frightening." Even as she uttered the words, Jennifer knew she was lying.

The two women parted ways. Jennifer went back to her apartment, and Simone drove to the Grand Hamilton Hotel. She requested the connecting suite to Charlie's room. Fortunately, it was available. She suspected Charlie kept that room empty at all times for her surprise visits. It was a game they played; reenacting the night they fell in love, the same night of Casey Bouvier's memorial. On that night, Charlie had reserved the connecting room to his, knowing Simone was going to be checking into the hotel for the Bouvier wedding. At the end of the evening, after a long day at work, he had knocked on the connecting door to her room. By her opening the door, she had opened her heart, and a pathway leading to the beginning of a heated and romantic love affair, that has grown deeper over the last year.

Now, once again in her room, she took a long luxurious bath, gave herself a pedicure and manicure, and ordered room service. She left behind the worries of home, and enjoyed the amenities of the Grand Hamilton Hotel.

Charlie did not know Simone was at the hotel that evening. A few times she put her ear up against the connecting door, and listened for sounds. Once she heard his television, she knocked on the door to his suite. Charlie opened it with trepidation, but his questioning look turned into a big smile when he saw Simone dressed in only a satin cami and shorts. His clothes were rumpled, he looked tired, but his eyes danced with excitement.

"Seeing you is the best thing that has happened to me today," he said as he embraced her in his arms. She fell safely into his arms.

It was eleven-fifteen, they were tired, but their joy at seeing each other after a stressful and arduous day, energized them.

"I need a shower," he said. "Can you order our special snacks?"

Simone called room service and requested a double order of fries, a bottle of Prosecco, and a glass of single malt scotch.

"Charlie," she said as they relaxed on the sofa, "we have to talk."

A flash of panic passed over Charlie's face. "I know from experience, Simone, that when a woman says that, it isn't good news."

"It's not."

"Are we okay?" he asked taking her hand in his, his face blanketed with concern.

"Yes. We're perfect," she said with a smile. Then, she blurted out, "I have a stalker. And he, or she, has been entering my house."

Charlie stood up, picked up the remote and shut off the opening monologue of a late-night host. He stood with his back to her, for what seemed a long time.

He turned and faced her. "How long has this been going on?"

"Several months ago, Jennifer and I went to Seattle for a wedding. After I returned, I discovered my underwear – my panties - were gone."

Charlie tried to keep his temper under control. "That was months ago. Why didn't you tell me sooner?"

"Charlie, please don't be angry. That won't help me. I need you to hear the full story. Then, I'll answer any questions." She continued. "After the underwear was stolen, I went to Jennifer's father's funeral."

"Yes, I remember."

"When I came home, I found dozens of roses in my kitchen. Then, today I played hooky and went home early to take a nap. Shortly after I woke up, I heard someone opening my front door. I hid under the bed, and the intruder stood inches from my face. He or she had on blue paper botties. I was so frightened, I decided to come here and spend the night. Charlie, may I stay with you until my team and I leave for Paris?"

Charlie paused, and exhaled a long breath. "I have so many questions, I don't know where to begin." He sat down across from her.

"First, of course, you'll stay here. Secondly, did you report this last incident to the police? The flowers you mentioned - are they the ones a client had sent you? And why didn't you tell me sooner?"

"Yes, the police know. No, the flowers weren't sent by a client, and I didn't want to worry you. But after today's invasion, I felt the need to tell you what was going on."

Charlie stood up, walked to the window, and seemed to be staring out into space before asking, "Do you suspect me?"

Now it was Simone's turn to be quiet.

Charlie turned and faced her. "You do."

"No, I don't suspect you, Charlie. I did in the beginning. I'm just confused. At first, I thought maybe you were playing a game about the underwear, and delivered the flowers as a welcome home gift. But when I told you a client sent me flowers and you didn't say they were from you - I knew they were from someone else. I'm sorry to have considered you a suspect."

Charlie sat down, and placed her hands in his. "Simone," he said with a tentative smile, "I think by now you know I would never do anything as creative as to steal your lingerie," he winked. "If the police thought I was a suspect, they would have interviewed me by now, so let's put that aside, and focus on who could be doing this."

Simone instinctively held back telling Charlie about the text messages. She never realized until now how difficult it was for her to completely trust someone. Was it memories of her father's abuse, or losing Joe, or just part of her personality? Her thoughts were interrupted by a knock on the door. "Room service."

Charlie quickly left, closing the connecting door between them. Although their romance wasn't a secret, he still needed to keep some sense of decorum, and not add fuel to his pending divorce. When the waiter left, Simone opened the door, welcoming Charlie back into her room.

They indulged in their traditional late-night snack of French fries. Simone enjoyed a glass of Prosecco, while Charlie savored a glass a scotch.

"Until you leave for Paris," Charlie reiterated, "I want you to stay here, or I'll stay with you at your place. You can't be alone."

"Thank you. I was hoping you'd agree."

Simone soon fell asleep feeling safe in Charlie's arms, while Charlie wondered who was putting her life in jeopardy.

The following evening, Charlie stayed at Simone's house, arriving after his evening class at Fairfield University. They were both exhausted, but had the energy for a night of passionate lovemaking.

"I love you so much, Simone," professed Charlie.

"And I love you."

They fell asleep in each other's arms.

Simone dreamed that her cell phone was ringing. She quickly realized it wasn't a dream at all. She swung her arm out to pick it up, and knocked over her bedside lamp. Charlie sat up abruptly and asked, "What time is it?"

Simone grabbed her cell phone. "It's one-fifty a.m."

The caller ID flashed, *Barbara Kemp*. She was calling from Paris.

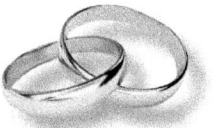

Ten

The streets of Paris were crowded with fast-moving shoppers and gawking tourists. The heat was usually less intense in late September, but this year, it seemed Paris was busier and hotter than ever.

Barbara slipped in and out of stores, buying gifts for her bridal party, her parents, and a wedding gift for Biff. *Biff,* she thought. *We've been together so long that I feel as if we're already married. Will a legal piece of paper make us happier, or is our mundane routine all that I have to look forward to? Is it normal for a bride not to care about the flowers, the food, the ceremony, or who shows up for the wedding? I hope Biff doesn't get drunk during the reception. He promised he'd stop drinking after we're married.*

Her thoughts dissipated at the smell of freshly baked croissants. Her mind, muddled with questions and hesitation about marriage, wafted away at the thought of a coffee and a freshly-made buttery dessert.

She asked for a table inside the cafe, away from the throngs of people, the noise of the city. She wanted to relax and enjoy her final days as a single woman. Once she settled in at her table, with a view of the bustling street, she chided herself. She was certain that every bride had these apprehensions.

Across from the open air café were three Parisian men leering at young teens, undoubtedly making suggestive comments. The girls, likely tourists, were wearing cutoff mini-shorts, and body-hugging tank tops. *Men,* thought Barbara, *they're all pigs.* Why didn't she consider that the girls' apparel was an open invitation for comments?

As Barbara scanned e-mails on her cell phone, she heard a waiter ask, "Voulez-vous une table?"

A brash blond in a revealing short dress with a plunging neckline, responded loudly, as if the waiter were deaf. "I don't talk French, but I'd like to sit here, in the sun."

"Very well mademoiselle," answered the waiter.

"Oh, you speak English. How nice for a Frenchie."

The waiter returned with a café menu.

"I don't read French. All I want is a coffee and one of those little semi-circle muffins."

"Do you mean a croissant, mademoiselle?"

"Yeah, one of those things," she drawled.

The waiter turned and did an exaggerated eye roll to the pastry chef behind the counter. He returned a few moments later with her order.

It's women like that who give Americans a bad reputation, thought Barbara. She put her head down to study her phone, but something about the woman seemed familiar. Barbara lifted her head and took a closer look. She reminded Barbara of someone she knew, but she couldn't figure out who. The lecherous men across the street complimented the mystery woman with whistles and suggestive stares. She smiled back at them, re-crossed her legs allowing her dress to slide up even more, and absorbed the catcalls with great pleasure.

"You whoo!" she shouted. "Over here."

Barbara, along with several other diners, looked up to see who she was calling. Barbara couldn't believe her eyes. It was Biff. He walked towards the café, leaned down kissed the blond bimbo, and sat down across from her. "Good to see you, Candy."

Barbara slid further down in her chair.

Sounds of disappointment emanated from the men across the street. They moved on to find fresh bait.

Candy had been Biff's girlfriend a dozen years ago.

Barbara asked to be moved to a table further back in the restaurant, hoping Biff wouldn't notice her with the sun shining in his eyes. She observed Candy's intimate friendliness towards Biff, occasionally touching his arm, and re-crossing her legs, exposing more thigh for Biff to enjoy. Barbara took a few photos of them with her iPhone.

To reaffirm her suspicions, she went onto Facebook and typed in Candy's name. There, Barbara saw photos of the bimbette in suggestive poses. She clicked on her Friend's list, and found Biff's photo. They'd been friends for four years, and there were several photos of Candy, in a skimpy bikini on Biff's boat. *That cheating bastard*, she said to herself.

The waiter approached, but Biff waved him off. Instead, he shared the croissant with Candy, and finished her coffee. He left some euros on the table, and the couple sauntered off. Barbara quickly dropped money on her table, and wiggled her way around the other tables to the street. By the time she got outside, Biff and Candy were lost in the crowd.

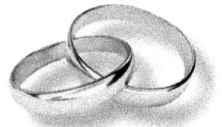

Eleven

"Hi, Barbara, what's up?" Simone said into the phone, trying to get her mind to focus.

"I'm not marrying Biff. He's a cheater . . . a jerk . . . a drunk," she said in between sobs.

"Calm down, Barbara. Where are you? Do you know what time it is?"

I'm in Paris. It's eight in the morning." She paused for a moment, as if checking her watch. "Oh no, Simone. Did I wake you up? I forgot you're six hours behind us. Sorry. But I have to tell you not to come to Paris. I'm not marrying that skirt-chasing, no-good, son-of-a-bitch cheater."

Simone heard Biff's voice in the background, "You're over-reacting. It was an innocent kiss."

"Barbara, I want you to go to another room, where you can talk to me privately, without Biff listening. Can you do that?"

"Yes. Biff can go back downstairs to the bar – his favorite room in the hotel," she shouted so loudly, Simone had to remove the cell phone from her ear.

"Barbara," Simone said sternly, "I need to talk to you, alone. Otherwise, I can't help you. Leave your room, find another place to talk, and call me back in five minutes. I'm hanging up now."

Simone got out of bed and apologized to Charlie for waking him up. She threw some cold water on her face, and headed to the kitchen to make a cup of strong coffee.

This was going to be a long, middle-of-the-night, frantic bride phone call. It wasn't the first one she had received, and certainly, it wouldn't be the last. Quite often brides develop pre-wedding jitters and call Simone for guidance.

"Tell me what's going on," Simone said when Barbara called her back.

"A few things: I found a receipt from Bloomingdale's in Biff's wallet. It said, ladies' lingerie." Simone didn't want to ask why she was looking through his wallet. Usually, when women did that, they didn't trust their man.

"So, what's so unusual about that? Maybe he purchased a negligée for the honeymoon."

"The receipt was dated eight months ago. A pair of my favorite underpants went missing around the same time. I always take them with me when we go away – they're Biff's favorite."

A chill ran through Simone. *Another woman with missing panties,* she thought.

"I stopped at an outdoor café this afternoon, and Candy showed up. She's one of Biff's old girlfriends. I think he bought the lingerie for her, and I wouldn't be surprised if he gave her my favorite pair of underwear. He's friends with her on Facebook; he's not even friends with me! They seemed very chummy when I saw them together today at an outdoor café."

Simone shifted subjects, "Could it all be a coincidence?" asked Simone. "Did Candy see you?"

"No. I was sitting in the back of the restaurant. Biff walked up to her table, sat down, gave her a kiss."

"Again, it could all be a coincidence. Did he look surprised to see her at the café?"

"No. It seemed like a planned meeting. He's cheating on me, that bastard."

"Don't jump to conclusions, Barbara. Many couples who have had a relationship in the past, reconnect on Facebook. Sometimes, the most troublesome situation is just an innocent coincidence." Simone did not believe in coincidences, but she wasn't going to say that to Barbara.

"I showed Biff the photos I took with my iPhone. He went pale. Then, he fessed up that he ran into her at our hotel, and suggested they meet to catch up. He swears he didn't know she was in Paris."

"Did you ask him about the Bloomingdale's receipt?"

"No. I don't want him to know I went through his wallet."

She let Barbara's response hang in the air. Shifting gears again, she asked, "Why did you say yes, that you would marry Biff?"

Barbara hesitated for a moment. "Because I love him. Well, I thought I loved him. Besides, I'm comfortable with him. We've been together for a long time, and at this point, I guess it's too late to turn back."

Simone had heard this same response from other brides. They felt they had come so far with wedding plans, and had invested so many years in the relationship that they couldn't reverse their decision. Too much money had been spent to turn back.

"Barbara, it is not my place to say whether or not you should marry Biff. I would not encourage you to get married just because of the amount of time, or money, you've invested. You know what's in your heart."

She heard Barbara sniffle. Simone continued, "Has Biff ever given you a reason not to trust him?"

"No," she answered quietly.

"To the best of your knowledge, has he ever cheated on you?

"No."

"Stayed out overnight without a good excuse?"

"No."

"Can you imagine your life without him?"

Barbara responded, "No."

"Barbara, you and Biff have been living together for five years, and dated for three years before that. You said he has never given you a reason not to trust him, so why now? Because you saw him with Candy? Or, are you afraid of the marital commitment?"

Barbara paused. "I guess you're right, Simone, I am afraid. Maybe it's all the excitement. Marriage is a big step, but deciding to live together, equally so. Biff and I are so good together. Our families are happy we are together. Sure, we have our minor problems, and things get boring at times. But who doesn't have issues? I can't imagine my life without him. Maybe, I *am* overreacting, and simply have wedding jitters. Thanks for listening, Simone. I feel better."

"That's okay, Barbara. Call me anytime. I'll see you in a few days. Until then, you and Biff need to have a good, honest talk. Will you promise me that you'll do that?"

"Yes," she responded, unconvincingly.

Simone's gut told her this marriage had a slim chance of surviving the next five years; she wasn't a trained marriage counselor, but she had good instincts when it came to couples.

Simone continued, "Discuss the things that are bothering you, Barbara. The two of you need to make a list. I call it the 3-D's. Discuss the things that bother you, decide on solutions or workable compromises, and then document the path to a better life together. Sometimes writing down each other's vows are powerful tools."

"That's a good idea. I know two things on my list," Barbara said with determination: "Candy, and Biff's drinking. He said he's going to cut back on his drinking after we're married. Maybe I can get him to agree to that in writing, so the next time he gets drunk, I can throw it in his face."

Simone chuckled, and said, "That's *not* the purpose of documenting promises. You're angry now, but once you step away, and see it logically, I'm sure it will all seem trivial." She wondered if her advice was in vain. "Remember, if you make a promise to Biff, and agree to it in writing, you don't want him throwing it in your face in the future. No, use it as a tool, not a weapon.

"Okay . . . I guess . . . Thanks again, Simone. Good night."

Simone went back to bed, and snuggled up to Charlie, who was still awake.

"You're more than a wedding planner, you're a Dr. Ruth," he whispered in her ear. "You were very patient, and logical. Can you be my wedding planner when I get married?" he teased.

"Good night, Charlie," Simone said with a chuckle. "I mean, good morning. Go back to sleep."

A few hours later, Charlie was shaking her awake. "Get up sleepy head."

"What time is it?" she asked through a yawn.

"It's nine o'clock."

"Thanks for letting me sleep. I needed the rest."

"I'll make us coffee." He left the bedroom and headed for the kitchen.

Simone got out of bed, and noticed her lamp was still on its side. She lifted it up, and placed in on the nightstand. A small round object dropped onto the rug.

"Charlie, please come back in here. Look what fell out of the lampshade."

"Is that what I think it is?" he asked, with trepidation.

Twelve

Simone didn't bother calling Chief Jacobs to tell her about the camera in the lampshade. She would tend to that later, after she got to work. The thought of having the officers back in her home was too much for this morning.

She searched Google for alarm companies in her area.

"The first opening we have is in three weeks," said the representative.

"Don't you have anything sooner?" Simone begged. She explained the break-ins, the camera in the lampshade, and that she was leaving for Europe in a few days.

"I'll speak to my manager." Simone was put on hold.

Simone put the phone on speaker, and listened to Muzak while she prepared breakfast for her and Charlie.

"Thanks for staying here until this gets settled," she said as she gave him a quick kiss on the lips.

"I wish I could stay with you until you leave for Paris. I'm very concerned about this situation."

"You're sweet." She didn't want to ignite another analytical conversation about her situation. She still had not told him about the text messages. The less they spoke about the elephant in the room, the better.

She went back to the stove and prepared breakfast. Charlie stood by the railing and looked out across to the beach. Gulls were bobbing up and down as they rode the white caps of the incoming tide. He watched a seagull soar up, drop a crab to the ground, and dive to retrieve his prey.

The breeze delivered a late-summer coolness. The setting was serene and peaceful, juxtaposed to what was happening yards away inside this house. *Who could be breaking into Simone's house,* Charlie wondered.

"Thank you," Charlie heard Simone say as she disconnected the phone call. "Good news and bad news," she announced as she joined him on the deck. "The owner of the company is coming within the hour. The bad news is, he's coming with his cousin, Jack, the locksmith."

"BCJ?" Charlie asked. They've taken to giving Butt Crack Jack that nickname.

"Unfortunately, yes. Apparently, Jack knows everyone in this area, and has installed locks and alarms in many homes."

"I'll protect you from scary Jack," Charlie said with a smile. "It's slow at the hotel today. Besides, it'll give Frederick an entry in his, 'Uncle Charlie Screw-Ups' notebook. Charlie pretended to be writing in a notebook: *VI showed up late today. Again.*"

Simone returned to the kitchen to finish cooking. Charlie shook his head at the thought of his nephew still wandering around the halls of the hotel. *Soon,* he thought, *I'll be out of that hotel and off doing a job more rewarding, and closer to Simone.*

"Breakfast is served," Simone announced, snapping Charlie back to reality.

They savored their breakfast of runny scrambled eggs (Charlie's favorite), buttery brioche toast, sliced sweet tomatoes from the local farm, well-done bacon (Simone's favorite), followed by additional cups of French roast coffee.

"I wish I could sit here all day, every day. This is so peaceful," Charlie said.

"Yes, it is. I feel very fortunate to have found this home . . . close enough to see the water, but far enough from hurricane destruction."

"Having the house lifted twelve feet, and installing breakaway garage doors was ingenious."

"That was all Pete's idea. He was, and still is, a great contractor."

"And a great lover, from what I've heard around town," Charlie teased.

"Oh, Charlie," Simone answered, blushing slightly. "Still jealous after all this time?"

"Always, my love," he said as he reached across the table, took her hand and kissed her palm.

The tender moment was interrupted by the sound of two panel trucks pulling up in front of Simone's house. One was Jack's, looking just as messy and dirty as the last time he was at her home.

"That's Jack?" Charlie asked as he watched him get out of his truck and lift his pants up over his enormous gut. The pants quickly slipped under the inflated fat.

"Jealous?" Simone teased.

Behind Jack's truck was another panel truck with the words, Aldo's Alarms across the side.

"I hope this doesn't take too long. I want to get to the office and finalize everything before Jennifer, Jonathan and I leave for Paris."

"Jennifer is going, too? I thought it was just you and Jonathan."

"With all that is going on, I can't focus on the wedding. Besides, the number of guests went up from one-twenty five to one seventy-five. I wouldn't be surprised if, by the time of the wedding, the guest list goes up to two hundred people. Things are much more relaxed in Europe. It's best if Jennifer comes along. She'll return with Jonathan, who I think is afraid of flying."

"Why do you say that?" Charlie asked, as they continued to watch Jack and Aldo remove their equipment from their trucks.

"He mentioned to Jennifer that he'd never flown before. He asked her what it felt like. So I think he'll appreciate having Jennifer with him to hold his hand."

Charlie and Simone walked from the deck, and opened the front door. The gate squeaked open while the two men climbed up to the front door. Handshakes and introductions followed. They stood on the front steps for a few minutes discussing outside cameras, and where they would be placed.

"I'd suggest you put a camera inside your house," suggested Aldo, as Jack went to get ladders. "The outside cameras pick up a certain radius. If someone came in through a side window, you wouldn't know. Or, if they saw the cameras outside, they might hide their face, not knowing there was a camera peering at them inside the home. Strategically placed, you'll be able to see someone walking around inside. And, I'd install a Ring Doorbell, alerting you when someone is at your door."

"I guess that makes sense," Simone agreed.

"I'll be right back. I have to get my equipment." Aldo walked down the flight of stairs, and stopped to talk to his cousin.

"I don't know if I want someone watching me . . . or us," Simone said.

"I thought you'd have control using your iPhone."

"I want the monitoring company to watch the house while I'm away for the next two weeks. Whoever is entering, seems to do it when I'm away. Or when they think I'm not home." A thought flashed through Simone's mind, but she couldn't capture the logic behind it.

Just then, the two men returned with ladders, tool belts attached, and boxed cameras. They placed everything on the stoop outside her door.

Simone wanted to reflect on her thoughts . . . something about what she just said . . . when they *think* I'm not home . . . but fear coursed through her body as she watched Aldo and Jack place blue paper booties over their shoes.

Thirteen

Simone and Charlie stared at the men's feet.

"Is something wrong, Ms. Simpson?" Aldo asked.

"Ah . . ." Charlie began to speak, but Simone cut him off, giving him a warning look for him not to say anything.

"Oh, no, nothing is wrong. It's just that most workers don't cover their feet when they're in someone's home."

She followed the men down the hallway, the familiar paper-scraping-the-floor sound behind her.

"From this angle, you would have a view of the front door, and the living room," explained Aldo. "Would you also like a camera inside your master bedroom?"

Simone thought for a moment. "Who has access to the video?"

"There are three different options," Aldo said. While Aldo explained the various plans to Simone, Jack's eyes scanned the inside of Simone's bedroom – his gaze stopped on her unmade bed. Charlie noticed this, walked past the trio, and closed Simone's bedroom door. Simone gave him an unspoken thank you smile.

"I'd like to be able to view the record of who was in my home. Who else, you said, will have access to viewing the cameras?"

"Only the monitoring company staff. If there is a forced entry into your home, an alarm will notify our monitors to access your account to see who's entering the establishment." This did not sit well with Simone. "We'll send you a text, or call. Otherwise, there's no reason for anyone to go into your account. We respect your privacy with the upmost professionalism."

"I guess that makes sense," Simone said reluctantly. "You can put a camera inside, but be sure it only monitors the front door and the living room. I don't want guests thinking they're being watched while in the bedroom."

Simone and Charlie sat in the living room reading the newspaper and occasionally watching the workers. Jack wore the same looking clothes he had on the last time he was there: dirty jeans, and a dingy yellowing tee shirt, too small for his bulk. Jack slowly climbed a folding aluminum ladder, causing it to shift and rock under his weight. When he reached the desired height, he removed a drill from his work belt with his right hand, and a camera base from his left pocket. As he reached up to drill a hole, his pants slid down, exposing his enormous hairy gut that hung over his tool belt, along with a cavernous hole for a belly button. His pants slipped even more. Charlie now understood what BCJ was all about. His gaze went to Simone's, and they stifled a laugh.

"I told you," she whispered.

"Gross." Charlie whispered back.

An hour and a half later, Aldo and Jack packed up their trucks with tools, and tossed their dirty booties inside. Aldo placed them into a Hefty garbage bag, and Jack tossed his shoe covers haphazardly into his vehicle. Simone looked deeper into Jack's truck and saw a collection of blue booties tossed on top of tools, contractor buckets, and on the truck's floor, along with empty fast food wrappers and soda cups. *What a slob*, she thought to herself. *How does he find anything in that mess?* "I wonder what his house looks like," she whispered to Charlie.

He nodded. "I'm amazed he has any business. He looks so unprofessional."

Jack hauled his mass of a body into his truck. The vehicle coughed and stuttered a few times before finally starting. He beeped the horn, stuck his head out the opened driver's window, and yelled, "I still say, ya should get a guard dog." He laughed, then drove off.

Simone, Charlie and Aldo watched his truck belch and rock as it made its way to Greens Farms Road, heading toward I-95.

"I have to apologize for my cousin," Aldo said. "He doesn't have many social skills. Grew up with folks who were more interested in gambling than taking care of their nine kids. He was the youngest . . ."

"May I have my bill?" Simone asked, cutting Aldo off from his saga of woes about Jack.

He handed Simone a packet of instructions on how to access the cameras, suggesting she download the app to her iPhone. "You'll be able to see what's going on all the time both outside, and inside. Most people don't log in, unless they have a pet, or if something happens. I'm sure you'll be fine."

Aldo got into his truck, and drove away. Unlike his cousin, he didn't beep his horn, shout suggestions, or drive a rundown, dirty truck.

"I don't like Jack," Charlie said. "I see why you thought he was creepy. The way he checked out your bedroom made me sick."

"Thank you for closing the door. There's something about him that makes me feel so uneasy." Shifting tack, she said, "I guess we should both go to work."

That evening, while Simone waited for Charlie to arrive after his class, she packed her bags for Paris. Occasionally, she looked up at the camera in the hallway, feeling as if a big eye was watching her every move.

And watching, it was.

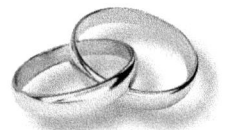

Fourteen

At his home, Jack went to his room located in the basement of the small home. This was his sanctuary, where no one else ever entered. Not even his mother, who lived upstairs, had a key to the locked door at the top of the stairs. She often warned him that if there were ever a fire, she wouldn't be able to get to him.

"Don't worry, ma, I'll crawl out the window," he snapped in a snarky tone. He and his mother knew, he would never get his fat body through one of the small, below ground well windows. This was his space, he was safe here to do his work. In case of an emergency, he'd leave through the Bilco doors that led to the backyard.

His desk matched the floor of his truck. Tools, a key-cutting machine, dirty clothes, and empty fast-food containers covered the space. The room had a stale smell of body odor. The windows were never opened, rather they were nailed shut, protecting his abode from invaders. At the back of the room was a small bathroom, with cracked, mold-covered tiles, and a mildew-covered, torn shower curtain. The bar of soap, sitting on top of a filthy sink was encrusted with body hair. The toilet hadn't been cleaned in years.

The only organized section of this dungeon was on the wall near the electrical box. There, in a neat row were keys hanging, like little metal soldiers. Each one was attached to a key ring, with the name of the home's owner and address written in small lettering. Every time he installed a lock, he made a copy for himself. Occupants never knew how many times he had invaded their premises.

Hanging on the walls in his self-made cell were photographs of women of all ages, sizes and shapes. Above his daybed, home to a sagging mattress stained with bodily-fluids, were his prized photographs of Simone: Simone in her car, Simone giving Pete a kiss on her front steps, Simone at the Porsche dealer, Simone leaving her office, and now, he'd be able to get photographs of Simone inside her house. He became aroused.

Jack had not known such exquisite joy and sexual excitement since he installed a camera for Dianna Delacroix, a runway model, lovingly called by him as, "My Double D's". And double D's she had. He didn't care if her breasts were filled with silicone or God-given. He dreamed they were filled with vodka, so he could suckle them until he got his fill.

Now, his new desire was Simone Simpson, a beautiful, sexy woman, who didn't appreciate how desirable she was.

He logged into his computer, and clicked on Simone's account.

"You will be mine," he said out loud to himself. "You will stand naked in front of me, bound and gagged, as I take care of my mounting desire. And you will watch as I pleasure myself, like I am now. Yes, Simone, you will be mine."

Fifteen

The three wedding planners arrived at JFK five hours ahead of their flight.

"Simone, why did we have to get here so early?" moaned Jennifer. "Ever since you got . . ." she stopped talking when she saw Simone's piercing stare, as to say, *Don't say anything in front of Jonathan.* Jennifer almost said, 'Ever since you got the cameras installed.' But she contained herself, and let the moment pass.

"You never know how bad the traffic will be going to the airport," Simone interjected. "I'd rather be early than miss our flight because of an accident on the road, and have to rush through security."

"I'm nervous," Jonathan admitted. "I've never flown before. Well, I did once, when we came to New York from Puerto Rico. But I was three at the time, and I don't remember anything about the flight."

"You'll be fine," Jennifer comforted. "I'll sit next to you and hold your hand. Don't look to Simone for sympathy, because you won't get any."

Simone looked at Jennifer, almost expecting her to stick her tongue out at her. She wondered why she often needed to zing her. At the Bouvier wedding, Jennifer got angry that Simone suggested she not go for dinner with the hotel security guard. Later that evening, close to midnight, Jennifer announced that their Los Angeles clients had canceled the wedding, only to have learned about it hours before their flight. It seemed Jennifer needed to 'get even' with people when she perceived to be slighted by them. Simone dismissed the thought as idiosyncratic.

They arrived in Paris on Wednesday morning, three days before the wedding. The flight was uneventful, and Jonathan survived his first transatlantic flight.

"Wow, that wasn't so bad," he said as they deplaned and extended their passports for inspection. "And I certainly didn't mind the view."

"You mean the pretty attendants," Jennifer said laughing.

Or, the stewards, thought Simone.

They gathered their luggage, went outside and hailed a taxi. They arrived at the Hotel George V in the heart of Paris.

Simone and Jennifer shared a room, and Jonathan was across the hall. On the day after the wedding, Jennifer and Jonathan would return to the States, and Charlie would move into Simone's room.

Before they left for the trip, Simone said, "Don't worry, Charlie. Jennifer and Jonathan will protect me. Besides, I'm in Europe, and the crazy person is in Connecticut. I'm not concerned. See you in a few days."

"Don't hesitate to call hotel security if you suspect anything," he said.

"I will. I promise," she assured him.

The hotel was convenient since the reception was being held at Le Cinq, the restaurant inside the Hotel.

On the day of the trio's arrival in Paris, a meeting with the bride and groom was arranged for eight o'clock that night. Because of the time difference, Simone suggested to Jennifer and Jonathan that they rest, meet at six-thirty for a light supper, followed by the meeting with their clients.

Barbara and Biff, who had made up, were staying at the same hotel. On Thursday afternoon, Barbara would go back to her family's estate, and stay there until the wedding, while Biff stayed behind. His bachelor party was scheduled for Thursday evening at a nightclub a mile away. He planned to sleep all day Friday, and be refreshed, and sober for the wedding on Saturday.

Simone called Barbara and Biff's room. "Hi Biff. It's Simone. We arrived a few hours ago. I'm confirming that we will be meeting tonight at eight o'clock."

"Yes, we're looking forward to seeing all of you again," he said. Biff moved his mouth up against the mouthpiece, and whispered, "Especially you."

Simone ignored him, and plowed forward. "I also want to reconfirm that your bachelor party will be tomorrow, and it has not been moved to

Friday, the night before the wedding. I've seen too many grooms - and brides - show up at their wedding with a hangover. I want you and Barbara to enjoy, and remember, your wedding day."

"I understand – not to worry, Simone," he said. He paused for a moment. In almost a slow and seductive whisper he said, "Thanks for caring about me."

"I'm just doing my job," she said, dismissing the added innuendo.

Feeling rejected by Simone for a second time, he snapped, "By the way, Jonathan said you won't allow him to come to my party. Isn't that being too controlling, telling him what he can, and cannot do? You shouldn't stop him from enjoying himself while he's in Paris," he said flatly.

"Biff, that's none of our business," Barbara chimed in, overhearing the conversation.

Keeping a professional voice, and ignoring his nervy comment, she said, "Thank you for inviting him, but he has to work tomorrow evening." She didn't have to answer to him. She plowed forward, "I'll see you and Barbara tonight at eight for a final review of the schedule."

Again, holding the phone close to his mouth he whispered, "I'm looking forward to seeing you again, Simone. You're easy on the eyes."

Simone was silent for a moment, ignoring his repeated flirtations. "Good bye," she said, and hung up. She concluded Biff was a man who wanted constant validation that women found him exciting and desirable. *How sad for him,* she thought. Maybe Barbara did have reason for not trusting him, and obviously, his flirting with other women wasn't on her list of 3-D's.

Simone, Jennifer and Jonathan met in the lobby at six-thirty, enjoyed a light supper, and then met their clients in the lounge.

"Nice to see you all again," said Biff. He gave Simone a hug and a kiss on the cheek, which did not go unnoticed by the others, especially Jonathan. Simone withdrew from his embrace, feeling as if she needed a shower.

"Let's get down to business," said Simone, taking the lead. On her laptop, she showed them three-dimensional views of the cathedral, the side rooms, and the altar. "We won't have time for a rehearsal, but it should be fairly straightforward. The church has an organizer who will walk you through all the steps. Jennifer will also be there to assist. Jonathan and I will tend to the vendors, making sure they all show up, and aware of what they need to do." They discussed the restaurant seating plan, reviewed the menu, and other matters relating to the big day.

"You're very organized and detail-oriented, Simone," Barbara complimented her. "You've thought of everything."

"Thank you, Barbara. During the next couple of days, my staff and I will be busy meeting with all of your vendors. You don't have to worry about a thing. Just show up at the Church by ten-thirty, and enjoy your wedding day. Until then, relax. Call or text if you have any questions."

They parted ways. The three planners were exhausted, went back to their rooms, and arranged to meet in the lobby at nine o'clock the next morning.

Sixteen

The next day, the three planners crisscrossed Paris, from one end of town to the other, introducing themselves to the vendors, and reviewing details. Jennifer's favorite was the baker, who gave them a taste of the wedding cake filling, and a box of madeleines. All the vendors spoke English, saving Simone from having to translate to Jennifer and Jonathan. In between, they had lunch at an outdoor café as they people-watched, acting like true Parisians.

They got back to their hotel on Thursday at five-thirty. They were exhausted, and on a sugar high from consuming the entire box of cookies. Everyone agreed to convene in the lobby at eight o'clock for dinner along the Seine. "I've made a reservation at one of my favorite restaurants," she told her co-workers. "You'll love it."

"Will I have to eat snails?" asked Jonathan, wrinkling his nose.

"Only if you're lucky," quipped Simone.

Jennifer showered, dressed, and put on her recently-purchased Garrice high heels. She announced, "I'm going for a walk. I need to break in my new shoes. I'll meet you in the lobby."

"I hope you'll be able to stay upright in those stilts," she joked with Jennifer. "I'd topple over after a minute."

"It's all in the balance, and luck," Jennifer said.

"I'll be down in ten minutes," Simone said. "I just need to finish my makeup, and put on my flats."

Jennifer left the room and headed downstairs. Meanwhile, Simone finished her toilette, and put on her shoes. Her thoughts traveled to Charlie. She couldn't wait until he arrived. She wanted to show him all the sights . . . sights she and Joe had shared long ago. The memories stopped her short. *Would I be imagining myself back in Paris with Joe, reliving our experiences? That wouldn't be fair to Charlie,* she thought. Simone was feeling confused, along with a deep sadness at the loss of her husband, whom she had met in Paris. She convinced herself she and Charlie would make new memories together.

As she fastened her second earring, there was a knock at her door, releasing her from her reverie. She looked at her watch. It was five minutes to eight.

She opened the door, expecting to see Jonathan. Instead, it was Biff.

"May I come in?" he asked, as he walked past Simone without waiting for an invitation.

"I'm about to leave for dinner," she said, uncomfortably. She didn't close the hotel door. Instead, she stood near the threshold. "What can I do for you, Biff?"

He staggered a little when he walked past her, his words slurring, "I came to talk. I've been thinking a lot about you, Simone." He turned and smiled at her, an evil look in his glassy eyes. "You don't respond to my words of admiration, Simone. Don't I excite you? I know you find me attractive."

Simone let these questions stay with Biff, and chose not to answer.

"Biff, I think you've had too much to drink. And you haven't gone to your bachelor party yet."

He stared at her, unsteady on his feet. A few seconds later, he took a step toward her and announced, "I like your house, Simone. It's so inviting being so close to the water."

A chill ran through her body. Her heart rate increased. Panic began to rise, but she reminded herself to stay calm and assess the situation.

"What do you mean?"

"Just what I said. I like your house. I like your Porsche. I like your beach. I like everything about you."

"How do you know about my house?" Her mind began to race. *Could Biff be the intruder? Barbara said she had a pair of her underwear missing. Could he have a panty fetish? The underwear went missing before we all met. How could he have gotten into my house? How did he know where I lived?* Questions, tinged with fear ran through her mind.

She tried taking stock of the situation, recalling her self-defense training. The only thoughts that ran through her head were, *This can't be happening.*

"Biff, you need to leave, or I'll call security." She thought of the promise she made to Charlie, that if she suspected anything, she'd call for help.

"No need for that," he slurred. "I just want a kiss. You know . . . kiss the groom . . . it's a tradition."

She ignored his request, and walked towards the hotel phone. Biff grabbed her right wrist and pulled her into his arms. His breath smelled of liquor. A horrible memory flooded her mind when her father's alcoholic breath had lingered on her hair for hours.

"I want you, Simone. And I know you want me. I see the way you look at me." He started shaking her like a ragdoll as she fought for her release.

"You're crazy," she yelled. "Let go of me, Biff. You're hurting me. Let go, or . . ."

"Or, you'll what? Playing hard to get really turns me on, you know that. Can you feel my excitement growing?"

Simone's memory of her father pressing his erection against her back flashed through her mind. Bile rose in her throat.

"Let go of my arm. Help!" He was too strong for Simone. She clawed at his fingers, trying to pry them off her wrist.

Biff stifled her mouth with his. She pushed his face away with her free hand.

"Help!" she yelled again.

"Shut up, bitch. You need to be controlled."

He tightened his grip on her wrist and raised his right hand to slap her across the face. She ducked, missing the slap. He staggered a little. As he concentrated on his balance, his grip loosened, enough for her to get a finger under his thumb. She wrapped her hand around the finger, and with all her strength, pulled it backwards. He gave out a yell, and he was down on his knees in seconds. Using her foot against his chest, she pushed him down to the floor, all the while continuing to pull his thumb out of its joint. She knew that if she let go, and tried to run, he would grab her leg, causing her to fall. She moved her foot down firmly into his crotch, while she continued screaming, "Help! Help me!"

At that precise moment, Jonathan rushed in. Equally strong as Biff, with an adrenaline rush fueling his body, he lifted Biff up by his belt, and shoved him towards the door. "Get out of here, you bastard," he screamed.

Biff fell to his knees, got up, and stumbled again. "Bitch," he yelled as he ran towards the elevators. "I hope you die," reverberated in the hallway.

Jonathan slammed the hotel door, another protective barrier against Biff.

"Are you all right?" Jonathan rushed to Simone, offering comfort. "Did he hurt you?"

She sat on the edge of her bed and inspected the red welts on her wrist. "I'm fine. Thank you, Jonathan. You showed up just at the right moment."

He didn't know if he should offer a hug, a shoulder, or his arm for her to hold. He kept a safe distance, trying not to invade her space. "I had a bad feeling about him the first day we met. I don't know how you and Jennifer deal with guys like him. I can't imagine his behavior at his bachelor party tonight. In hindsight, I'm glad I'm not going. The man is an animal." He paused, contemplating. "I think you should say something to Barbara. She should know what she's marrying," Jonathan suggested.

"No, I'm not sure I'm going to tell her anything. I think she knows what sort of man he is. I think she feels she's come this far, it's too late to walk away now. Denial is a strong defense mechanism."

She continued, "There are three sides to every story, Jonathan."

"Three?" he asked his head cocked to the side questioning.

"His side, my side, and the truth," Simone explained. "I think Barbara will choose to ignore all three."

Simone stood up. She contemplated telling him what Biff had said regarding where she lived, but she decided against it. She would discuss Biff's actions with Jennifer later that evening, when they're back in their room. Maybe she *should* tell Barbara, after all. But when . . . just before walking down the aisle?

"Let's go for dinner," Simone said while rubbing her wrist. The welts were disappearing. She would never again put herself in a position of being alone with that menacing animal. "I'm happy you were here to rescue me."

"You looked like you were able to take care of yourself. I heard about how Jennifer took down Hathaway. You women are scary," he said jokingly.

Simone remembered the scene when the Greenwich, Connecticut police tried to arrest Robert Hathaway, who had killed Casey Bouvier, hours before her wedding. He was a security guard on the grounds of the Grand Hamilton Hotel. Hathaway had put Jennifer in a chokehold and placed a gun against her temple. Jennifer used her self-defense training to take down Hathaway, at the precise moment a bullet flew by Simone's head.

Jonathan gently put his arm around his boss' shoulder and gave her a tender hug. Hoping he didn't cross a boundary, he quickly removed his hand. The hug was followed by a big smile.

There was that twinkle again.

Seventeen

Jack laid back on his daybed, his sexual urges satisfied. He dozed, dreaming of Simone. He assured Aldo, "I'll monitor Ms. Simpson's home once a week. I'll view the digital record, making sure there aren't any problems with the feed. Just as I do for Ms. Delacroix, and the others in the area."

None of Aldo's customers had problems with break-ins. A few had their alarms tripped by burglars, who quickly left the premises when the alarm blared. He mumbled, "Don't worry, Simone. I'll take care of you."

He knew that Simone was out of town, overhearing what she had told Aldo about going to France. She'd be returning tomorrow night. Jack waited until one-thirty a.m., and drove his mother's fifteen year old Nissan to Simone's house. When he was a block away, he parked the car, turned off the engine, and used his iPhone to remotely shut off Simone's house cameras. Dressed in black slacks, a black shirt, and a black knit cap, he walked to her residence. He was sure that everyone in the neighborhood was asleep.

He had brought a can of WD-40 with him for the squeaky gate. He recalled hearing that sound the previous times he was at her house. During the quiet of the night, Jack couldn't risk the noise waking a neighbor. He walked slowly up to Simone's house, bent down, and quickly sprayed the squeaky gate with the lubricant. Then, he placed the can in a bush, where he would retrieve it on his way out.

Quietly, he climbed the steps, and rang the doorbell, in case someone was house sitting while she was away. He rang it again. When no one answered, he used his key and unlocked her door. *These women think getting a lock from a big box store is going to protect them,* he thought. He slipped inside, took a deep breath, calming his pounding heart.

He kept the house lights off, and used the castoff glow from the streetlights to guide him to Simone's bedroom. He looked through her closet, placing his face against her clothes, deeply inhaling her body's scent.

He removed all of his clothes and stood naked inside her closet, surveying her garments, shoes and accessories. He removed a Diane Von Furstenberg wrap dress from a hanger and placed it around his body, barely covering his large belly. He rubbed the dress against his sweaty, hairy body, with extra rubbings against his genitals. He found a long strand of pearls and put them around his neck. Rummaging through her makeup table, he carefully painted on lipstick, blush, and mascara. Then, he sprayed White Diamond perfume onto his chest. *Oh, I'll be smelling you tonight, my lovely one.* He admired himself in the full length mirror.

He looked through Simone's dresser drawers, admiring her bras and panties. His sexual arousal stirred again when he held up a pair of her purple thong panties. He put them against his face and smelled the fresh scent of fabric softener.

He had to control himself for fear that he would ejaculate onto her fine dress. He took off the dress, and the pearls, then placed them back where he thought they belonged. Naked, Jack walked into the bathroom, shut the door, and flipped on the light. He turned on the faucets, bent over the vanity and grabbed the bar of lavender soap. He roughly washed his face.

His arousal mounted as he smelled Simone's perfume on his bare chest, inches from his nose. Residual soap burned his eyes as he groped for the hand towel, and dried his face. His thinking was becoming muddled as his sexual arousal increased. He splashed cold water on his face and head in order to quell his excitement.

Then, he folded the face towel in half and placed it back on the towel bar. Before he shut the light, he looked at himself in the mirror and grinned. He was satisfied.

He remotely turned back on Simone's cameras with his iPhone. He saw his naked body on the small screen. His lips formed a large grin as he waved to himself, knowing the camera was aimed at her bedroom, and not the front door as originally agreed. He remotely shut off the cameras again, hoping Aldo didn't check the feed. He had strategically aimed the camera to capture Simone's coming and going from her bathroom. If he was lucky, he would get flawless photos of her naked body. He felt his excitement rising again. *I have to get out of here.*

He had considered placing a discrete camera inside her bedroom, but was afraid if it was found, she would suspect him. Someone had previously planted a camera in her bedroom, which had initiated the emergency call to Aldo. He wondered who else was watching Simone. A jealous rage began to boil. Then, he remembered the man who was with her when he installed the cameras. *Charlie. Yeah, that was his name. Who was he? She told me a boyfriend didn't have a key. I'll monitor the cameras . . . If he touches her . . .*

Eighteen

Biff's bachelor party didn't disappoint the attendees. There was heavy drinking, abundant cocaine and strippers. Biff got his sexual pleasure from one stripper in particular. He spent most of the night openly fondling her ample breasts and equally ample backside. He didn't care if the other guys saw him; in fact, he encouraged them to share the 'booty.' It was an all-out orgy. This was his last night of freedom, and he was going to enjoy himself.

He hoped Simone didn't tell Barbara about his earlier actions. He would say that it was Simone who came on to him. He wasn't going to worry about that now. At this moment, he was having the time of his life.

He returned to his hotel room with a woman on his arm at three in the morning.

"You're amazing," he told her. "You're not afraid to do anything. Barbara is a bore in bed, she would never allow me to do these things to her."

"Anything you want, Biff. Anything for you," she cooed.

Physically exhausted, he got out of bed for a drink of water. His head was pounding with a hangover. He noticed an ice bucket on the table, a bottle of champagne sitting in the cold water. Alongside the bucket was a plate of cookies. *Nothing like a little 'hair of the dog,'* he thought. He popped open the bubbly, and took a long guzzle from the bottle. Then another. He released two loud belches, and mumbled, "That's better." He removed the plastic wrap from the small dish, grabbed two cookies, consumed them quickly, and got back into bed.

"Hey, wake up. I'm ready to go again." But his companion was sound asleep. He whispered, "You want to make this man a happy bachelor . . . one more . . . time . . . hey, wake up . . ." But he never got to finish his sentence. Biff gagged, gasped for air. He wrapped his hands around his throat as agonizing blisters swelled inside his mouth, cheeks, and lips. He felt his face and eyes swell, as if his skin was going to explode. He clawed at his neck as his windpipe closed off the airflow, chocking him. His breath ceased as he clamored for air. He grabbed the bedside phone, but it fell out of his hand, and banged against the nightstand until it hit the floor.

"How may I help you, Monsieur Bradshaw?" the voice on the other end said. Only inaudible gagging sounds were heard, followed by the banging of the phone.

"Monsieur Bradshaw? Monsieur, are you okay?"

Moments later, the hotel manager and two security officers were pounding on his door. Not waiting for an answer, the manager used his passkey to open the hotel door. He flipped on the lights, waking Biff's companion. She screamed when she saw the men standing over the bed.

"What's going on?" she yelled, holding the bedsheet up under her chin. "Who are you? What's happening?"

"We received a call from Monsieur Bradshaw," said the manager. "He sounded distressed."

One of the security officers looked at the manager and shook his head as he removed his fingers from Biff's carotid artery. The phone's receiver lay on the floor, a loud beeping sound filling the room.

Biff's blank eyes were wide open and his swollen tongue protruded from his mouth. His face was twice its size, making him unrecognizable.

Biff Bradshaw was dead.

Realizing she was lying next to a dead body, the woman emitted another scream. She jumped out of bed, and gave everyone in the room an eyeful of her naked body. The hotel manager, and the two security guards, slowly absorbed her body, before the manager said, "Mademoiselle, please, dress yourself."

The Paris Police Prefecture arrived within minutes, as well as a hotel doctor and a medical examiner. Biff's friend, now fully dressed, asked if she could leave. "I'm sorry, Mademoiselle, you will need to stay for questioning."

"I'm not supposed to be here. He's getting married tomorrow. I was just . . ." her heavy accented voice trailed off as she began to cry.

The officer asked, "And what is your name, Mademoiselle?"

"Cunningham. Candy Cunningham. I'm an American."

Nineteen

Someone was banging on Simone's hotel room door. Jennifer stirred in her bed.

"Who is it?" Simone said, her voice raspy, her throat parched from the dry air in the hotel room.

"It's Jonathan, Simone. Open the door. This is an emergency."

Simone quickly grabbed a hotel bathrobe, wrapped it around herself, and opened the door.

"I'm sorry to wake you up. Biff Bradshaw is dead."

"What?" Realizing what Jonathan said, Jennifer bolted up in bed. "Biff is dead?"

Simone froze at the words, remembering Casey Bouvier, who, a year before, died on her wedding day. "Is this some sort of joke?" Simone asked. "Because if it is, it isn't funny." She motioned for him to come in. "What time is it?"

"It's six. I was in the lobby, and saw a lot of commotion. Someone said a groom died, and the police were coming . . ."

"Hang on, Jonathan. I can't process anything. Before you tell me what happened, I desperately need coffee. Simone picked up the hotel phone.

"Yes, Mademoiselle Simpson, how may I help you?"

"Room service, please." She ordered a continental breakfast for three people, with extra coffee. "Merci."

Jonathan discretely averted his eyes as Jennifer got up and put on her robe. She sat on the edge of Simone's bed to hear the full story.

"Okay . . . slowly . . . what happened?" Simone asked, rubbing her eyes, trying to focus.

"I went to the lobby for a magazine, and I noticed a big commotion. The manager told people to leave the area, and a few of us got ushered into the café. The doormen stopped people coming in the front door. It was mayhem. I saw lots of police, an ambulance, and a truck with a French sign, 'coroner.' The police took someone out of the building in a black bag. It was awful, Simone. I hope when I die, I'm not put in a black bag like that."

There was a knock at Simone's door. Room service arrived with a basket of buttery croissants, a selection of jams, soft cream butter, and a carafe of piping hot coffee. Simone poured a cup for Jonathan, one for Jennifer, and one for herself.

"Go on," Simone said, grabbing a croissant and stuffing it in her mouth.

"I saw the same woman at the registration desk whom I spoke with last night. I asked her what was going on. She said a groom died. I asked her, 'Bradshaw?' She nodded her head and said, 'Oui.' Then she put her index finger to her lips, and said, "Shh."

"In the lobby, I saw a woman walking with the police. She was crying and wearing a policewoman's coat over her skimpy clothes. It looked like Bradshaw brought home one of the women from his bachelor party. I know it wasn't Barbara. Maybe he died of a heart attack during sex."

Simone wondered if that woman was Candy, whom Barbara saw Biff with at the outdoor café.

"I wonder if Barbara has been informed," said Simone. "Let's get dressed, and sit in the lobby to wait for Barbara. Jonathan, we'll meet you there in ten minutes. She and Jennifer dressed quickly, agreeing there wasn't enough time for a shower, just a face wash and teeth brushing.

In the lobby, Simone conversed in French with the hotel manager, asking for information, as the wedding was to take place the next day.

"I'm sorry, Mademoiselle Simpson, I'm not at liberty to tell you what has happened here today. I understand you are the wedding planners assigned to the Bradshaw wedding, but until we have contacted the next of kin, we cannot say anything further. Once we are at liberty to discuss the situation, I will let you know."

"Merci, Monsieur. Je comprends."

Simone was not going to be the one to inform Barbara. She, Jennifer and Jonathan would just have to sit and wait, either for a phone call, or for Barbara to arrive at the hotel. She instructed her team to settle in until the manager called for them.

Thirty minutes later Barbara, her parents, and Biff's parents entered the hotel. Simone instructed, "Wait until Barbara approaches us. We need to stay out of this situation as much as possible."

The families were quickly escorted to the manager's office. Simone wished she could be a fly on the wall. They emerged shortly after with Barbara leaning on her father's arm. She lifted her head and saw Simone sitting across the lobby. She ran to Simone, holding her closely.

"Oh Simone. It's just awful. Biff died in bed with that woman he was with at the café. They think he had a heart attack."

"I'm so sorry, Barbara," Simone said with as much sympathy as she could muster. "How terrible for you, and your family. Please, tell me what we can do for you."

Barbara ranted, "I told you - I knew he was cheating on me. He deserved to die," she said with malice in her voice, her slate blue eyes wide with anger. "I'm glad I found out now, instead of marrying the bastard."

"Barbara, I'm so sorry," were the only words she could mutter. She wasn't about to agree with the bride, or tell her what had transpired with Biff the night before.

She continued. "I will be in Paris for the next few days. If there is anything you need, don't hesitate to call me. My team and I will notify the church, the restaurant, and the vendors involved. Would that be okay with you?"

"Yes, please. I'm sorry you got involved in this mess," Barbara apologized.

"I'll take care of the wedding items. You should be with your family. You need each other. And Barbara, be kind to Biff's parents. It's not their fault their son cheated on you."

Barbara paused for a moment to reflect on Simone's words. "Thank you. You're right. I'm so angry right now, I probably would have taken it out on them."

"I'll send you an updated e-mail later. Don't worry about anything right now, except taking care of yourself." They hugged again.

"Thank you Jennifer, and Jonathan," Barbara said between newly formed tears. "I don't know if I would have been able to get through this without all of you." She turned and walked back to her waiting parents.

After the two families left the hotel, Simone turned to her team, fully in control of the situation, and announced, "Back to work. We have to revisit all the vendors, and cancel the contracts. We'll start here with the restaurant."

Simone looked up the manager of Le Cinq on her iPhone, and noticed she had missed a text message from last night.

Are you having fun in our city of love? Joe

Twenty

Although the vendors spoke and understood English, canceling a contract required a command of the French language. Jonathan and Jennifer stood by taking translated notes. It was arduous, but they had to be sure every service provider understood the cancellation, and Simone's team had to understand the financial impact on Barbara.

"It is not the first time, Mademoiselle," said the manager at Le Cinq. "Unfortunately, the food has been ordered and delivered, so we can only refund a small portion of Mademoiselle's order. We will not charge her for the alcohol, as it has not been consumed. But our cost for the food . . . I'm sure she will understand."

"Yes, I am sure Mademoiselle Kemp will understand," Simone said in perfect French. She continued, "We'll need confirmation in writing, of course, as to her expenses, which I will present to her. As you can imagine, she is quite distraught, and she cannot deal with the matter. I'll give you my company's credit card, and I'll arrange reimbursement from Mademoiselle Kemp."

"Of course," said the restaurant's manager. With a heavy accent he said, "I am quite impressed you are willing to take on such a task. Mademoiselle Kemp is fortunate to have you working for her."

Giving Simone a closer look, he added, "Do you intend to stay in Paris much longer, Mademoiselle Simpson? It would be my pleasure to show you the intimate parts of our lovely city."

Simone knew what he meant by the word intimate.

"Thank you, Monsieur, but my fiancé is arriving tomorrow, and I will be seeing Paris with him."

"But, of course, Mademoiselle."

When they left the restaurant, they got into their rented car, and headed to the photographer's studio.

The barrage of questions ensued: "When did you and Charlie get engaged? When's the wedding? Where's the ring? Can I be your wedding planner?" asked Jennifer.

"Yes, when did that happen?" asked Jonathan. "Can I come to the wedding, too?"

"He was kind of cute – for an old guy," Jennifer added.

"Cut it out you two," Simone said with a smile. "Charlie and I didn't get engaged, there's no wedding, and yes, he was kind of cute for an old guy." They all laughed.

Simone continued, "French Men 101: Don't tell them you're single. That means you're unattached and they have a chance of getting you into bed. Don't tell them you're married, because that means you're bored with your husband as a lover, and they have the challenge of winning you over, and making you stray. Do tell them you have a fiancé. They will back off thinking you're having lots of sex and don't need any outside stimulation."

"Thanks for the lesson, teach," said Jennifer.

The photographer was understanding, and asked his sympathies be extended to the families.

The florist said she would separate the flowers, and sell them as arrangements. "What's left over, will go to the hospital where they'll brighten everyone's day."

"No charge for the cake," said the baker. "I can sell the tiers separately." This time they left the bakery with a box of madeleines, macaroons and a baguette.

While they stood by their car, Simone said, "All we need now is a cheese shop and a wine store, and we'll be set for lunch." They found one two doors away.

They drove to Tuileries Gardens and enjoyed a relaxing picnic. "Paris at its best," said Simone.

When they returned to their room, Simone composed an e-mail to Barbara, explaining the actions they had taken:

Dear Barbara,

We met with the vendors. They were kind, understanding, and extend their sympathies. All said, 'no additional charge' above their initial deposit, except for Le Cinq. They will not charge for the unconsumed alcohol, but must charge for the food that has been delivered.

My company will forgo the 'day of' wedding service fee, but will still need to invoice for our travel, and the hours spent related to the wedding. I will send you a more formal letter in two weeks.

We extend our deepest sympathies to you during this most difficult time. If you need anything, please don't hesitate to call me.

Warm personal regards – Simone, Jennifer and Jonathan

Jennifer and Jonathan were craving a tour of Paris. Since the wedding had been canceled, they had Saturday afternoon and evening free. Simone obliged, with some trepidation, not knowing how she would feel revisiting the sights she and Joe had enjoyed together. Valiantly, she took them to the top of the Eiffel Tower, The Louvre Museum, and other prominent attractions in Paris. They ended the day with dinner and a boat ride down the Seine. They returned to the hotel well after midnight, tired, but high on the splendor of the Parisian lifestyle.

"That was an incredible day, Simone. Thank you so much," said Jonathan. "I can see why it is called the City of Love. Speaking of love, I see the sales clerk who checked us in, and told me about Biff. I'm going to see if I can get me some Paris-love," he said with a big smile. Simone thought, *all he had to do was show that twinkle, and she would succumb.*

"Good luck, Jonathan. Just be ready for the ride to the airport tomorrow morning. Good night."

"Doesn't that woman ever sleep? She seems to always be here," Simone observed. "Strange. She was here when we checked in, Jonathan said she was here at six this morning, and now, at midnight?" Her thoughts wandered.

"Do you think he'll get lucky tonight?" Jennifer asked as they rode the elevator up to their room.

"He doesn't know Parisian women," Simone said. "They love being in love. I hope he doesn't break her heart. Or, she, his."

"She'll probably chew him up, and spit him out. She looks like a tough cookie," joked Jennifer. "Come to think of it, this is the first time I've ever heard Jonathan express an interest in a woman. Honestly, I thought he was gay."

"Me, too," Simone agreed. "He's never mentioned a woman, or a man, in his life. As you know from experience, Jennifer, I prefer to keep our private lives separate from our drama-filled professional life."

Jennifer paused a moment, and added, "You know, Simone, it feels good you're there when we have personal issues going on. You're a great friend and boss, as well as a humanitarian."

"It's the wine talking, Jennifer," Simone teased. "But thanks. I have to say the same about you. You know a lot about my personal life, and you've never gossiped to Katy, Jonathan, or others in the office. And that means a lot to me."

Simone continued, reflectively, as she counted the numbers in the elevator cab. "I was bullied when I was in school, the other girls whispered about me to each other. It's hard for me to trust people not to spread unfounded rumors. I sincerely hope you're not offended by my wall of secrecy."

"Not at all," she sighed. "But, before we become two weepy dishrags, let's get some sleep. I hate to admit it - my new shoes are killing my feet. My bed is calling me, but so are my bags, which I have to pack for our flight home tomorrow," Jennifer whined.

Twenty-One

The following morning, Jennifer and Jonathan climbed into Simone's rental and headed to the Charles de Gaulle Airport, sleepy and sad to be leaving Paris.

After their bags were checked, they settled in at an airport bistro. The three enjoyed a delicious and hearty American-style breakfast of eggs, bacon, toast and home fries. Jennifer and Jonathan's flight was delayed for two hours, which was beneficial to Simone, as she planned to remain at the airport, and wait for Charlie's flight, due in a few hours.

"So, Jonathan, how was your midnight rendezvous with the hotel staff person?" Jennifer asked, with a slight tease in her voice.

"She had to work for another two hours, and I was tired, so I gave up. We promised to write." He paused, then added, "That's not going to happen, is it?" They all burst into laughter. "Seriously, Paris was magical, Simone. I will always remember the Eiffel Tower, and the feeling of romance in the air. Thank you again for including me in this trip."

The women looked at each other. Jennifer mouthed, 'Romance?'

Reflecting on the past few days, Simone was sad that Biff died, but relieved to no longer carry the burden of telling Barbara about his aggressive behavior the night of his bachelor party. Would she have encouraged Barbara to marry him? But it wasn't relevant, now that he was dead. She sympathized with the family. They'll have to figure out how to get Biff's body back to the States, and complete the paperwork involved. Emotions and confusion would be abundant.

Simone left Jennifer and Jonathan after they went through security. "I'll text you when we land in the States," Jennifer promised.

Simone walked to the gift shop, where she purchased a lusty romance novel, Seducing Harry: An Epicurean Affair. She found a quiet table in the corner of the restaurant, and immersed herself in the revelry of the book. Simone looked forward to a few hours of not dealing with texts from a dead man, but rather descriptions of luscious foods, with provocative sex scenes. She couldn't wait to get Charlie back to her room.

Two hours later, she heard the announcement that Charlie's flight had landed. She gathered her belongings and hurried to the gate. Moments later, he walked through the doors, a garment bag over his broad shoulder, and a smile so large, it told the entire story. She was equally happy to see him. He pulled her into his arms, and kissed her with unabashed passion. "I've missed you so much, my love," he said.

"And I, you." She began to cry. The last few days had been non-stop work, an emotional rollercoaster playing tour guide, culminating with Biff's death. "Tears of happiness," she assured Charlie. "Let's go back to the hotel. You must be exhausted after your flight."

"I slept most of the way, so I'm not tired. Did Jennifer and Jonathan leave?"

"Their flight was scheduled to leave an hour ago."

"Show me Paris, Simone. Show me the City of Love."

"I'll show you some love," she teased. "You won't want to leave the room."

They climbed into her rental, and headed back to the hotel to drop off Charlie's luggage before she gave him a tour.

While they drove, Simone's phone chimed announcing the arrival of a text message.

"Can you grab my phone from inside my purse, and read the text to me? I didn't check to see if their flight took off. I hope we don't have to go back to the airport to get them."

Charlie read the text, but remained mute.

"What does it say?" She quickly glanced at him. His face grew pale as he stared at the cell phone screen. "Charlie, what's wrong? What does the text say?" Simone's stomach started flip-flopping, her heart beat increasing. "Charlie?"

"It says,"

Please, don't take your lover to our secret places in Paris.
With my undying love, Joe

Twenty-Two

"Simone, what is going on?" Charlie demanded, furrowing his thick eyebrows.

She had pulled off the highway, and was sitting at a rest station. She didn't answer him. Instead she watched the rows of cars lined up at the petrol pumps, the people entering and exiting the building for the rest rooms, and the inside of the small, and busy convenience store.

With a stern voice he continued. "First, you keep it a secret that your underwear was stolen, and that you received dozens of flowers. You didn't want to tell me about the intruder until you were frightened for your life. And then, you found a camera planted in your lampshade. But this . . . this text message is beyond frightening. Is this from your stalker? Is this from someone who knows more about you than I do? Are you telling people that you wish you were with Joe instead of me?"

As calmly as possible, she answered him. "Charlie, now your fantasies are running rampant."

"Well, whoever sent you this text message knows you're in Paris with me, has a key to your house, and leaves you flowers." Charlie's voice exploded in anger. "Are you seeing someone else? Is there something you need to tell me, Simone? Do you have another lover? Was there something more you neglected to tell me the night you stayed at the hotel?"

The questions shocked Simone. "Of course not. There's no one else in my life, except you." She turned with a reassuring look. "It's complicated, Charlie. It's just complicated."

"Well, I'm not sure I believe you, Simone. Could it be you're playing a game with my affections? That you just made up the story about the panties, and bought the flowers for yourself? Maybe you had a friend send this text so that I would see it and get jealous. I'm not a game player, Simone. Eve played games, and look where it got us. Did you invite me to Paris just to torture me?"

Simone's anger was also escalating. How could Charlie even think like this? Her mind was shutting down, blocking him out. She wasn't willing to discuss this now. She turned away from him, refastened her seatbelt, and started driving towards the hotel.

"Can we talk about this?" Charlie asked.

"No. Not now," her green eyes flashed. "I'm too angry. Let's get you settled at the hotel." They rode for the next thirty minutes in silence.

In Simone's room, Charlie suggested they not leave, but have food delivered. "We need to get this settled, Simone. Please, let's not spend the next week angry with each other. That would be a waste of our time and emotions. I'm going to take a much-needed shower. Please, order some food. I'm starving."

Simone was equally annoyed and confused. A jolt of fear ran through her. Her thoughts were jumbled. *Who was sending the text messages? Why did Biff say he liked my house? He's dead, he couldn't have sent the text message. Is it possible there was a way to postpone sending a text until a later time, like you can with e-mails? Maybe Biff wrote the text, and scheduled it to arrive the day of his wedding. That didn't make sense. Could Barbara be in on it? Maybe this was a sick joke between her and Biff.*

Simone picked up the hotel phone.

"Yes, Mademoiselle Simpson, how may I help you?"

"Room Service, please." A memory flashed through her mind, that when she had ordered breakfast yesterday, the operator also knew who she was. She dismissed the thought; she had probably said who she was, and just didn't remember.

"Room service. How may I help you, Mademoiselle Simpson?

"Yes, I would like two hamburgers deluxe, two Coke-a-Colas, and a pot of café au lait. Thank you."

Charlie showered, dressed and walked out onto the terrace. He was wearing faded jeans, a light blue polo shirt, and Docksiders sans socks.

His hair was damp from the shower, a slight scent of soap emanated from his body. Although Simone was angry, her feelings softened when she saw how sexy he looked.

He leaned against the terrace railing overlooking the rooftops and narrow streets of Paris. To his left, he could see the flying buttresses of Notre Dame. Below, the streets were quiet, as many Parisians were home with their families on a Sunday afternoon.

Simone joined him, also silent, still not ready to go to battle. Charlie's jaw was set. The tension between the couple was palpable. She realized that this was the first time they had had a disagreement, and she wasn't helping the situation by being stubborn. There was a knock at the door. "Room service."

Simone signed the check, and the waiter pushed the cart out onto the terrace. "A lovely setting for dining," he said to Charlie.

Charlie didn't acknowledge the young man. He was too busy stewing to be pleasant.

"Merci," said Simone as the waiter took the receipt and left the room.

She sat down at the patio table, removed the silver cloche from her food, and took a bite out of her juicy hamburger. Charlie continued looking out over the balcony. She popped the soda can, poured the bubbling beverage into a tall iced glass, and dumped a large dollop of ketchup onto her fries. "Aren't you going to eat?"

Without answering her, he turned back to the table and sat down. Simone thought he must be as ravenous as he was angry. He ate his burger and fries with gusto, not lifting his head saying a word, or looking at Simone.

"Are you ready to talk?" she asked.

"I don't know. Maybe. Unless, you still want to keep everything a secret."

"Charlie, I didn't think it was your problem. You have a lot on your mind right now: work during the day, school at night, a divorce, your father, the hotel. I just didn't want to add to your problems."

Charlie hesitated before answering. "Do you really think you don't matter to me? Or, that what goes on in your life, doesn't affect me? I don't care about all those other things, Simone. I care about you. Was it your plan to never include me? What I don't know, won't hurt me?"

"I planned to tell you. Actually, I was going to tell you when we were relaxing in Nice, and I had more time to think this through."

"If I hadn't seen the text message, would you have told me about it?"

"Yes. And before you ask, I've told the police. I'm not taking this lightly, Charlie. They have started an investigation on who might be sending the texts."

"Texts? There have been others?"

"Yes. Apparently, they're being sent from a burner phone."

"Do the police think it's the same person who broke in?"

"They said that would make the most sense. It could be someone close to me; who knows my schedule, who has access to my house . . ."

"So, you suspected me?" he interrupted.

"To be honest, at one point I did. Just like I suspected you took my underwear and left the flowers. You know a lot about me, including my husband's name."

"Simone, a lot of people know your husband's name. All you have to do is Google your name. How about Jennifer? Jonathan? Katy? Maybe Katy's son. He's a teenager, and they do crazy stuff. You said he's starting college; maybe it's a hazing project. How about your cleaning lady?"

"Google . . . that's interesting . . . I hadn't thought about Google . . ." her thoughts wondered off as the pieces started fitting together.

"Well, have you thought about those people?" Charlie demanded again.

"I thought about all of them, Charlie. But I have no idea how any of them could get a copy of my key. Only my cleaning lady has a copy of the new key. And she's been with me for years. I trust her. I don't keep a duplicate in my office, or under my door mat, or in a flower pot. And they would have had to make three copies: the first time when my underwear was stolen, then when the flowers were left, and then after placing the camera in the lampshade."

"Is there anyone else you can think of who would be doing this?"

"Yes, there is, but there isn't."

"That doesn't make sense," Charlie said before shoveling a bunch of fries in his mouth.

"Well, Charlie. There is something else I need to tell you. I'm afraid you're going to be upset."

"At this point, nothing will surprise me, Simone."

Simone took in a deep breath. "Remember my client, Biff Bradshaw?"

"Yes, the guy who got married yesterday."

"Well, he didn't get married. He died instead."

Charlie's eyes widened. "I don't know what to say, other than, what happened? When? Where? Why didn't you tell me this before I left for Paris?"

"I don't know. I was so wrapped up with canceling plans," Simone explained. "Things were moving quickly. We had to visit all the vendors, and by the time we got back to the hotel, it was too late to call you. It was horrible to see Barbara and her family so distraught. It reminded me of the Casey Bouvier wedding."

"It seems people die around you," Charlie uttered spontaneously.

Simone got up and walked away from the table, her eyes filling with tears.

Realizing his insensitivity, Charlie moved to her side. "I'm sorry, Simone."

After a few moments she lamented, "Joe died in my arms."

"Simone, I'm truly sorry. I didn't mean anything by that statement." Charlie wrapped his arms around her. She turned and buried her head in his embrace, as tears stained his shirt. "You know I didn't mean it the way it sounded."

"I know," she said. "But people around me do die." She began to sob.

Charlie reached over to the table, grabbed a cloth napkin and wiped her tears, holding her close. "I'm sorry, Simone. I'm sorry I hurt you."

She inhaled his manly scent, and felt his solid chest and arms around her. She felt safe and protected. But she also felt the wall of protection beginning to grow around her heart. Charlie's words hit a soft spot, as people around her did die.

The sun was beginning to set. The evening's activities commenced. Horns honked as cars jockeyed their way through the narrow streets of Paris.

They moved from the railing and sat down at the patio table, her emotions settling a bit.

"Are you able to tell me what happened, Simone?" asked Charlie.

Simone began, "The initial report was that Biff died of a heart attack, but they'll know more after the autopsy. Apparently, he was in bed with Candy, his former girlfriend. Remember when Barbara called in the middle of the night because she saw Biff with Candy sitting at an outdoor café?"

Charlie nodded.

"He told Barbara he and Candy serendipitously ran into each other at the hotel, and met at the café simply to catch up. But it appears she was there at his invitation. I don't know the details, and I'm staying out of it."

"That's smart," Charlie muttered.

"But I think he had something to do with breaking into my house."

"How does he fit in with your house being broken into? You hadn't met him until months later."

Simone explained. "Biff came to my room on Thursday, a bit intoxicated. We got into a discussion, and he said he liked my house, my car and the beach." Simone left out the part about the assault, and Jonathan's rescue. It wasn't the time to add to the drama. "He made me think he could be the culprit. You mentioned Google, Charlie. Maybe he Googled me, checked Google Earth and saw my house and my car. I don't know. There's no way he could have sent the last text because he was already dead. Maybe he had one of his friends send the text as a joke. I'm very confused, and I'm still trying to figure it all out."

He took Simone's hand, and gave her palm a gentle kiss. "What about us, Simone? I love you, and want to be with you." His soft brown eyes teared. "But you keep pushing me back, and you have so many secrets. I don't know what to think."

"Charlie, I'm sorry. Because I've lived on my own for so many years after Joe died, I covet my independence. I didn't tell you because I didn't want you to worry. I've been so busy with my business, dealing with changing my lock, my car problems . . ." She stopped talking for a moment. "Charlie, they're all excuses. The truth is, I'm afraid of getting close to you because . . ." She hesitated.

"Why, Simone?"

". . . Because, I'm afraid you'll die."

"Oh, Simone," Charlie said. He lifted her from her seat and held her in his arms. "I'm not going to die. At least not now."

They stood on the terrace in an embrace, watching Paris unfold before them.

Twenty-Three

Simone and Charlie enjoyed the rest of their meal. The sun had set over Paris, there was a cool breeze, and she and Charlie seemed to be back to their normal rhythm. She felt their relationship was stronger on the other side of their argument.

Simone poured herself a cup of coffee, and unwrapped the complimentary dish of cookies. She noticed a warning label taped to the plastic covering written in several different languages: *Some of our sweets may contain traces of nuts and nut oils, or may have been made in a facility with other products containing nuts.* She removed the wrapper and grabbed a cookie. "Hmm," said Simone as she devoured a buttery cookie sandwich filled with a delicious chocolate spread.

"Will you show me the sights of Paris tomorrow?" Charlie asked her as he, too, indulged in a cookie. "Are you okay taking me to the same spots where you and Joe went?"

"I'm fine. It did feel strange when I took Jennifer and Jonathan to the top of the Eiffel Tower, and to Notre Dame. But not as upsetting as I thought it would be. They were my trial run."

"Are you sure you're okay with taking me to the same places?"

"We'll make our own memories, Charlie. I promise. When we go to Nice, let's do a side trip to Chartres Cathedral, and Monet's home. I have never been to those sites, so it will be something new for me."

Simone's phone suddenly rang.

"Must you answer it?" Charlie asked.

"Let me see who it is. I never did check on Jennifer's flight." Simone scanned the cell phone screen. It was Barbara Kemp.

"Good evening, Barbara. How are you?

"I'm doing as well as expected, given the circumstances. I received your e-mail. Thank you for canceling the contracts. I will settle with you once I'm back in the States. I can't think about that now."

"There's no rush. I put all the charges on my company card, so you only have to write one check to me. We'll meet after we're both back. I won't be in my office for another ten days. I'll send you a final invoice then."

"Thank you, Simone. You've been an incredible support. I would never have been able to take care of all the details without you."

Simone didn't want to turn this into a long conversation. She switched gears. "What can I do for you this evening, Barbara?"

"I have an update for you. Apparently, Biff did not die of a heart attack."

"No? What did he die of?" asked Simone.

"Anaphylactic shock."

"Oh, my," said Simone. "Do they know what caused it? Did he eat or drink anything he was allergic to?"

"Biff was allergic to hazelnuts," Barbara explained. "He was extremely careful, to never eat anything with nuts. He had an Epipen with him, but it never got used. The medical examiner found traces of cookies in his mouth."

"That's terrible, Barbara." Suddenly, a thought crossed her mind.

"The police found a plate of cookies in his room. A few were missing."

Simone's mind started to race.

"Candy said she didn't notice cookies in the room when they . . . well, you know."

Simone ran back to the terrace and grabbed the plastic wrapper. She handed it to Charlie, pointing to the ingredients.

Barbara continued. "The hotel has meticulous records on all their guests, their allergies and preferences, down to what type of soap they prefer."

"Yes, I remember when I checked in, we were asked questions about allergies, and sensitivities to soaps and room deodorizers. I had never been asked those questions when checking into a hotel. It's a very exclusive service," Simone interjected.

Barbara continued, "When he, or any guests of the hotel picked up the phone in their room, their names and room numbers appear on the computer monitor, along with any allergies. It is a sophisticated system. So if Biff had ordered cookies from his room, they would have been aware of his nut allergy, and would have inquired about the order. They might have recommended madeleines, which are made on premise, and do not contain nuts. Trusting the hotel, he would have eaten the cookies without questioning their content. Unfortunately, the cookies in his room were filled with a chocolate spread that had hazelnuts in it."

"Nutella," said Simone flatly.

"Yes, Nutella," parroted Barbara.

"I'm a little confused, Barbara. If the hotel computer system showed he was allergic to hazelnuts, why did they deliver cookies with Nutella to his room?"

"He didn't order the cookies. Someone else did. Simone, I think Biff was murdered."

"Are they sure? Do they really think he was murdered?" she said looking at Charlie.

Charlie shook his head.

Barbara continued. "They know the request was made on Thursday night. It could have been one of the wedding guests, or someone at his bachelor party. There are a few people who were jealous of Biff, and his family's money. And my money, too. Maybe they thought he'd get only a mild reaction and show up at his wedding with hives, but not this. It's hard to believe someone would have murdered him."

She paused for a few moments, then added, "Since the wedding was canceled, a lot of the guests switched their flights, and went home. It might be impossible to track down the killer. The hotel is interviewing the staff on duty that evening to see if anyone remembers a food order for Biff's room."

"Barbara, if someone ordered cookies from one room, to be delivered to another room, wouldn't the list of allergies be checked?" asked Simone.

"The list of allergies only shows up for the person placing the order from that particular room, not to where the food is being delivered. Since the kitchens are busy, between room service and the restaurants, it's hard to keep track. The waiter, who delivered the food remembered the time as a little after midnight. The room was empty. He left the chilled champagne in a bucket, along with a dish of assorted cookies. The order was charged to Biff's room. The hotel is going through their phone log to see which room placed the order. Or, it might have come from a lobby phone."

"Could the order have been placed by someone at the bachelor party?" asked Simone.

"Whenever someone calls from outside the hotel, the calls go directly to the operator. Calls from the operator to room service would be nominal. That was an easy check. No calls were forwarded to the kitchen."

Barbara continued. "No, Simone. The order was placed from inside the hotel," Barbara said emphatically. "The cookie delivery was intentional. Biff was murdered."

Twenty-Four

Simone and Charlie spent the next three days touring Paris. They awoke early, walked to a nearby café where they enjoyed robust coffee and freshly-made buttery bakery items. From there, they returned to their room, showered and dressed for a full day of sight-seeing. They hired André, a chauffeur who drove them to numerous tourist attractions including the Eiffel Tower, the Latin Quarter and Montmartre. One afternoon, André drove them one hundred kilometers to Giverny, where they spent hours touring Claude Monet's home.

"I've always wanted to come here, Charlie, but never had enough time. Isn't it lovely?"

"Peaceful, is more like it. I actually feel I've left my troubles back in Connecticut. I feel free. Does that make sense, Simone?"

"I think that's what vacations are for," she replied.

They stopped for lunch at a neighborhood eatery, and invited André to join them for the meal, and then again later in the afternoon, for rejuvenating cups of coffee.

"Tell us about yourself, André," Simone asked.

André explained in broken-English about his struggles raising his family with France's unemployment rate of over 10%. He lived thirty kilometers outside of Paris, and most of his money was spent on petrol.

"I have a wife and three small children. My mother lives with us. She helps Angela with the children, and the farm. My training is as a pastry chef, but large industrial bakeries have settled near Paris, and have lower prices. Restaurants don't need to pay for an independent pastry chef, like myself, so I am out of work. Tourists help the restaurant economy, but once they are gone, many restaurants have to close. Chauffeuring tourists is the only job I could find. I charge a little less than other drivers, and I give the concierges tips in order to get the better jobs. Money talks."

André passed around photos of his wife, children and his widowed mother. "We have a large farm with chickens, ducks, and two pigs," he said, as they viewed images of the family's vegetable garden. "Unfortunately, we have two male pigs, so no babies," he laughed. "We hope to have enough money before the winter to buy a female pig."

André appreciated Simone's knowledge of French. When he got stuck on a word or two, he would say it in French, and Simone would translate.

"Often, a tourist would holler words at me in English. They think I am deaf because I speak a different language."

The three of them laughed, Simone promising they would not yell at him.

He was happy to be serving a couple fluent in both French and English, who showed him respect. It was rare to be invited to lunch.

"I hope you will join us for lunch and afternoon coffee every day we are touring," Simone graciously offered.

"Oh no, Mademoiselle, you mustn't. That is intruding on your time as lovers."

Simone giggled. Was it obvious that she and Charlie were lovers?

"Nonsense," said Charlie, "we insist."

"Merci beaucoup," he replied, his head lowered feeling slightly embarrassed.

Over the next three days, André drove them to his favorite neighborhood haunts, where they indulged in enticing dishes of fresh fish, vegetables, and sinful desserts.

"I think my clothes won't fit after these meals," Simone said. "André, thank you for escorting us to locals' restaurants and sights. This has been wonderful."

"My pleasure," he responded in English.

At the end of their time together, hugs were exchanged. Simone told him in French, "Please, André, if you ever have the occasion to come to America, look us up. Here's my card. Charlie works at a hotel, and

he can get you a good price on a room." Simone didn't want to reveal Charlie's position at the Hamilton Hotel. It wasn't her place to give away free nights. "And this is for you and your family." In an envelope were Euros, the equivalent of $500 in American money.

"Mademoiselle, Monsieur, I cannot accept this. This is too generous. You bought me lunch . . . this is too much."

"Please take it. Buy a female pig," she said, laughing. "It is our way of saying thank you for four wonderful days in Paris. We will never forget our time here. Or you. May you have many blessings in life."

On their way to Nice in Simone's rented car, they stopped at Chartres to see the magnificent, multi-steeled, French Gothic cathedral. Afterwards, they found a small grocery store where they purchased cheeses, pâté, cured meats, a container of bitter olives, and several bottles of mineral water. They found a secluded hillside, put down a blanket on the grass, and enjoyed a quiet picnic.

Simone explained the text messages in more detail, the attack by Biff, and other secrets and fears she'd been keeping from Charlie.

"No more secrets," she promised. "I'll tell you, immediately, of any future home invasions or texts."

The weather in Nice was glorious, with temperatures in the low 80s, and cooler in the evening. The tourist rush at the middle of September was over, and the locals had returned to a more tranquil and relaxing environment. Charlie and Simone swam in the sea and took a deep sea fishing trip. They went on long walks into town, bought some souvenirs, and promised each other to come back again.

Dinners were just as spectacular, with fresh fish from the ocean, and garden grown vegetables. A creative chef served a meal with food shaped into quenelles. The appetizer had duck liver paté; the main course was fish of the day poached into the creative shape, including mashed potatoes and broccoli soufflé; and dessert consisted of ice cream and chocolate pudding.

They spent five days relaxing and enjoying the seaside town, and never wanted to return to the hustle and bustle of work back in the States.

Twenty-Five

They landed at JFK at five thirty p.m. They retrieved their luggage, and found their limousine driver waiting for them outside the terminal. Simone felt as if she had been away for a month, and not for only two weeks.

The driver put their luggage in the trunk while Simone and Charlie climbed into the back seat.

"Want me to stay with you tonight?" Charlie asked. Simone was looking out the window at the New York City skyline. Memories of her first visit to Manhattan on her way to New York University, years ago, flashed through her mind.

"Simone, did you hear me?" asked Charlie.

"Sorry, I was daydreaming. Your offer is very sweet, but we have to drive past Greenwich on our way back from the airport. You should get a good night's sleep in your bed. Besides, your father would want to see your smiling face early in the morning. Thanks, but now that I have the cameras, I feel safer."

Charlie asked the driver to raise the privacy glass, so their conversation would remain sequestered. Although, Simone had learned from the numerous limousines she hired over the years, some cars are equipped with a secret speaker in the driver's area. It was a safety feature.

"Have you checked the security feed?"

"I couldn't check it while in Europe, or in flight," she answered. Simone dug in her purse and took out her iPhone, tapped on the app, and was able to see outside and inside her home.

"That's funny. I thought the inside camera was aimed at the front door, but it seems to have shifted direction, and it's now facing my bedroom. I'll have to call Aldo in the morning, and ask him to come by and fix it."

She entered the dates she wanted to view, and things seemed uneventful. She saw that Anna Maria had cleaned the house.

"There must have been an electrical storm yesterday," she said to Charlie. "There's a one hour period where the feed is blank. I'll ask Aldo about that as well."

"If you feel uncomfortable, let me know. We can go directly to your house," Charlie said.

"I'm sure everything is fine. I'll look for the boogie man in the closets and under the bed."

"Text me when you get home, and let me know that everything is okay."

"I will," she promised.

"This was a wonderful trip, Simone. I secretly wish it had been our honeymoon."

"Charlie . . ." Simone started to say, ready to scold him.

"I know . . . I know . . . you're not ready. Soon, my love. Soon."

Charlie kissed Simone as he got out of the car. "Remember, text me when you get home."

He shut the limo door and watched it pull out of the estate, and head toward I-95. Charlie turned and faced the façade of the Grand Hamilton Hotel. *A far cry from Chartres,* he thought.

When they arrived at Simone's home, the driver moved quickly to remove her luggage from the trunk. Then he opened the passenger door, and helped Simone exit the car. He swung open the gate, and motioned for her to proceed up the steps in front of him. As she said, "Thank you," she suddenly stopped mid-way up the stairs.

"Is something wrong, Miss?" he asked.

"That's funny. That gate used to squeak."

"Maybe it's the humidity, Miss."

"No, that can't be it. It always squeaked when opened."

"Maybe a neighbor, tired of hearing the squeak, sprayed it with oil," he assured her.

She smiled, and wondered if Pete had stopped by and took care of the noise. He was known for making minor repairs. Once, he saw one of her gutters hanging loose. He fixed it, and didn't even bill her.

Simone opened her front door and flipped on the lights.

"Do you want me to stay, and make sure you're safely inside?"

She wondered if he had listened in on their backseat conversation. "Thank you, but I'm sure I'll be fine."

"I don't mind waiting until you check," he said standing by the entrance.

She had promised Charlie and Chief Jacobs that she would never again walk through her house without lights on, and go directly to sleep. Her false sense of security had gotten her into trouble in the past. She took a quick look around, didn't see roses on her kitchen counter, or any glaring evidence of an invasion.

"Everything looks good," she said. "Thank you for your concern."

The driver nodded, and made his way back to the limo. She closed the door after him. Then locked it.

The house was quiet and peaceful. Anna Maria left a small succulent plant, along with a note:

Doesn't need much water. Hope you had a good trip.
Look inside your icebox. AM

Simone smiled at the note, especially Anna Maria's reference to an icebox. She didn't seem old enough to remember one of those. Like Pete, she was often doing small, special things for her. She walked to her refrigerator and was jubilant to find Anna Maria had stocked it with Half and Half, a loaf of her favorite potato bread, fresh eggs, orange juice, cheese, and a large Pyrex dish of homemade lasagna. Simone realized she was starving, and chopped off a big piece of lasagna, placed it in the microwave, and was settled down on her sofa watching television. She picked up her phone to text Charlie, just as a message brightened her screen:

Are you home? Everything okay? Read the text from Charlie.

Everything is fine. Anna Maria left me a tray of lasagna, having late night snack. See you tomorrow night. Love you.

Good night. Love you too. Replied Charlie.

Simone watched the ten o'clock news as she devoured the lasagna. She discovered she had missed so much that was happening in the United States, both politically and socially. She decided she couldn't fix the world, and headed to her bedroom.

She glanced up at the camera on the interior wall, outside her bedroom. To help her feel less vulnerable, she closed her bedroom door, blocking the view from the one-eyed monster.

She wasn't tired now, refueled by the lasagna, and the euphoric memories of her time with Charlie. She decided to unpack before going to sleep. She opened her suitcase, grabbed her laundry, and walked inside her closet to toss the clothes into the hamper.

Suddenly, she stopped short. The clothes fell from her hands onto the floor. Someone had been in her closet. Her clothes were not hanging the same way she had left them. Her favorite wrap dress was sliding off its hanger, and it smelled of her White Diamonds perfume. Her pearl necklace was on a hook shared with another long necklace. Simone prided herself on her organizational skills, both at work and at home. She ran to her underwear drawer. All of the underwear was there, but her purple thong was rolled up in a ball and shoved in an empty spot. Misplaced.

The lasagna rumbled in her stomach. She felt dizzy . . . faint . . . her heart pounded. She raced to the bathroom and splashed cold water on her face. She reached for a towel, when she noticed it was askew, with a stain of lipstick and the remains of makeup.

"What the hell is going on?" she screamed out loud.

Twenty-Six

Simone hit the panic button, summoning Aldo, Jack, and the police. She texted Charlie:

Police and Aldo on their way. Someone was here.
Don't come. I promise to keep you updated.

Charlie texted back: *I'm on my way.*

Simone thought of arguing, telling him to stay put, but decided she really did want him with her. Then she called Anna Maria.

"Hello?" Anna Maria said with her usual accent, sounding a bit startled.

"Anna Maria," Simone cried into the phone. "I'm sorry to call so late, but I need to ask you something."

"What's wrong, Simone? I do something wrong?"

"Oh no. I just need to know if you noticed if the dresses in my closet were moved, or that the bathroom towel had makeup on it? Did you see anything out of place?"

"I was there two days ago, in the morning. I no see nothing. I go in your closet, and I wash your laundry. I no see nothing wrong. I wash your towels, too. All clean. Someone come into your home again? Police come here, talk to me again?"

Simone heard the panic in her housekeeper's voice, and felt sorry she was pulled into the drama, again. "Yes, Anna Maria. Someone came into my home. Don't worry about the police, they won't call you. I had cameras installed and I can see when you were here to clean. Again, I'm sorry to call so late. By the way, thank you for stocking my refrigerator. You're an angel. I'll call you tomorrow. Thank you."

"Shit!" Jack yelled aloud while driving to Simone's house. "I bet I screwed up. I knew I should have been more careful. Shit!" He violently slammed his hand on the steering wheel, causing the dilapidated truck to jump the sidewalk. He backed up, got the truck back on the road and continued on to Simone's house.

He recapped in minute detail when he was last at Simone's home: He remembered hanging up the dress, putting the pearl necklace back on a hook, and the thong back in the drawer. He had put the makeup and perfume back in their place. He put the towel back on the towel bar after washing his face. No, nothing would give him away. His secret was safe. A satisfied smile crossed his face.

Unfortunately, Jack was a notorious slob, and never considered that the extremely neat and organized Simone would notice something out of place.

Upon hearing the doorbell, Simone ran to open the door. It was the police. Shortly afterwards, Aldo's truck pulled up with Jack's right behind it.

The officers entered her home, and asked Aldo and Jack to remain outside. "This is police work. We'll let you know when we need you," said the officer. He closed the door in Aldo's face, just as the words, "We can see . . ." But the officer wasn't interested.

Aldo turned to Jack. "Did you see anything strange on the feed?" he asked his cousin.

"No, nothing. It was a little fuzzy last night, but nothing that lasted long," he lied. "I saw her cleaning lady there the other day. That's about it."

"She hit the panic button . . ." said Aldo while he scratched his head. "What could she have found that would cause her to do that?" He sat on the top step of the porch, contemplating. Then, he asked his cousin, "Did you install a camera in the back of the house?"

"No," Jack answered. "You never said nothing about a camera in the back."

"Come on, let's see if someone got in that way."

There was a Dutch door in the back of Simone's home, with a simple push button lock. "Well, that's a big oversight. She changed the lock on her front door, but didn't pay attention to the back door. And who puts a Dutch door on the back of the house unless you live on a farm? This lock could have been opened with a credit card," Aldo announced, priding himself in solving the mystery.

Simone and the officer saw the two men at the back door. "What do you want? I told you we have work to do," the officer said reprimanding them.

"I just wanted to point out that this door has a simple push button lock. Anyone could have opened it."

"And there ain't no cameras back here," Jack added.

Simone fumed. "Stupid," she snapped. "How stupid."

"I'm sorry Ms. Simpson," Aldo interjected. "I'm sorry we didn't see if there was a back door."

"*I'm* the stupid one," she said. "I completely forgot about the back door. I never use it, and I never imagined anyone coming or going through it. I enter and leave through the garage, or the front door. I have to walk through the pantry and past the washing machine to go out this way, then walk around the front of the house to get into the garage. My housekeeper does my laundry, so I never come back here. Now I understand why Chief Jacobs kept saying, change your 'locks', which confused me, because I only have one lock on the front door."

"It's a common mistake, Ms. Simpson," the police officer said in a comforting voice.

Exhaustion and anger took over. Turning to Aldo and Jack she said, "You're fired. Both of you. If you were competent, you would have known to look for a back door. Cancel my contract right now, and remove those damn cameras immediately. Especially that one," she shouted as she pointed to the eyeball outside her bedroom.

The two men scurried back to their trucks, returned with ladders, and twenty minutes later, had the cameras and equipment packed up, and were gone.

Meanwhile, a second policeman drove up.

"While 'dumb and dumber' are removing the cameras," she said to the police officers, "I'll show you what I found." She went into her closet and pointed to the dress that was slightly askew. "And it smells of perfume."

As she was about to remove the hanger from the rod, the policeman stopped her. "Don't touch anything."

She stopped. "The pearls don't belong on that hook," she explained as she pointed to an empty hook on the long row of small dowels.

The officers were impressed. "Most people wouldn't notice if something was out of place."

"I pride myself on organization. It's my way of controlling things, when situations are out of my control." She thought of the sexual abuse by her father, her husband's death, and how she lost him and her baby, among the many other tragedies over which she had no control. She opened her dresser drawer and showed him where the thong was shoved into the corner.

"We'll hold these items as evidence, and bring them to the lab." The officers put on latex gloves, and stowed the items, one by one, in large clear envelopes, and placed them on the dining room table.

"There's one other thing." Simone pointed to the bathroom. "The towel in there has makeup on it." That, too, was placed in an evidence bag. "And the bar of soap," she said with disgust, pointing to it.

The perfume, and all the items on her dressing table were added for analysis. "We should have preliminary results within seventy-two hours. If, whoever came into your house has a record, we might get a hit sooner."

"Simone." Someone shouted from the front door.

She left her bedroom, and ran into Charlie's arms.

"Are you all right?" He pulled her into an embrace.

"I am now." She never wanted to leave the comfort or safety of his arms again.

Introductions were made to the officers, followed by explanations of what had happened. Simone assured the police that Charlie would stay with her, and she'd be fine.

As soon as they left, Simone poured a glass of Pinot Grigio for herself, and a glass of scotch for Charlie, and brought it to the sofa.

"Want some lasagna?" she asked.

"Maybe later."

She relayed every detail to Charlie: the back door lock, the cameras, and how she fired Aldo and Jack. "I hope I never see the likes of them again. Now, I need to find a good security company. Meanwhile, I'll buy a nanny cam for my bedroom."

"Simone, the person who came into your house probably saw the cameras in the front, and somehow got in through the back door. I can't see how they would have gotten into your bedroom closet or bathroom without being detected."

"Remember I told you that there was some fuzz in the feed last night? Maybe that's when the intruder entered and was able to manipulate the system so they wouldn't be recorded."

"Who, besides you had access to your account?"

"Aldo and Jack. They said they would monitor my service until I became familiar with it, especially while I was out of the country."

"Do you think one of them could be the culprit?"

"That's an interesting thought, Charlie. I never did like Jack; something about him concerned me. He was the one who installed the camera outside my bedroom, which brings me to another thought: the inside camera was supposed to face the front door. Instead, it was aimed directly at my bedroom."

Charlie glanced up at the empty space on the wall. All that remained were notches in the sheetrock.

"I think you should call the officer who was here tonight, and give him Aldo and Jack's contact numbers. Maybe they've broken into other customers' homes."

Simone agreed. She placed a call to Officer Vern.

"Vern, here."

"Hello, this is Simone Simpson. You were just at my home."

"Yes, Ms. Simpson. Is something wrong?"

"No, everything's fine. Charlie and I were going over the details, and I think you might start your investigation with the two security men who were here earlier. We think one in particular could be the culprit."

Twenty-Seven

A quick search through the police database showed Jack "Jacques" Miller was questioned in the past when a neighbor filed a complaint that he was lurking outside her bedroom window. He had installed locks at her home shortly after she moved in. Jack claimed he was outside smoking a cigarette. She wanted him arrested for voyeurism. Since she had no proof, and a cigarette butt was found crushed near her window, no charges were filed. Jack was given a warning, and the woman never saw him outside her home again.

Another voyeurism complaint was filed against Jack two months ago. He had also installed new locks, and a security system at this home. This time, he was caught looking through a window, seen by the owner's young child, who ran and told her mother that a man's face was up against their living room window. The woman recognized Jack, and called the police. When questioned, he claimed he had dropped a tool while working at the home, and was looking for it. He produced a screwdriver from his back pocket, claiming he found it in the bushes where he thought he had dropped it.

After waking up a judge at two-forty a.m. to obtain a warrant, the police converged on Jack's home. They noticed Jack's truck was parked in the driveway. The house was dark except for a light emanating from a well window. Two officers rang the doorbell, then knocked loudly, shouting, "Police, open up."

At the sound of the banging, the light in the well window went out.

"Hey, Sarg. The light in the basement just went out. I'll cover the back, in case someone makes a run for it."

An elderly woman with white wispy hair opened the door a crack. She wore a chenille bathrobe that she clutched tightly under her neck. "Yes, what is it?" she asked.

"Police. We have a warrant. Open the door."

"Let me get my son. Just a minute, please."

"I'm sorry ma'am, please step aside." The officer pushed open the door slowly, and entered.

His radio crackled, "We have a runner."

Jack had snuck out through the basement door, and was making a run for it down the street, tightly holding a laptop under his arm with one hand, and his pants with the other. His excessive weight prevented him from getting very far. He had to stop to catch his breath.

"Don't go any further," the officers said as they caught up with him. "You're wanted for questioning." One officer grabbed the laptop as the other clapped handcuffs on Jack. They walked him back to the police car, and placed him inside.

"What are you doing with my son? He's a good boy. He didn't do anything," cried the elderly voice from inside the home.

"He's not under arrest, ma'am," the officer said trying to comfort her. "We're just going to bring him to police headquarters and ask him some questions. How do we get to the basement?"

"That door," she pointed. "But it's locked. My Jack keeps it locked all the time."

The officer kicked in the door, splintering it beyond repair, and made their way down to the basement. The sergeant stopped, and said, "Christ, what kind of a perv lives here?"

Plastered on the walls were photographs of women, in various stages of undress. Some photos were of the same woman sitting at a Starbucks drinking coffee with female friends, intimate positions with lovers inside their bedrooms, naked in the bathroom, driving their cars. And then there were photos of Simone getting into her car, kissing a man on the cheek on her front steps, and with Charlie walking along Compo Beach. And there was more: a photo of Jack wearing the dress that was askew in Simone's closet, along with various photos of him naked standing under the doorframe of Simone's bedroom. He had superimposed Simone performing lewd acts.

"This is sick," said one of the officers. Photographs were taken, and items were collected as evidence.

"Oh, my. Oh, my. That's not my Jackie's pictures. He would never do that. He's a good boy," his mother cried. A female police officer stepped forward and escorted her back upstairs, where she comforted the old woman. While the frightened woman sank into a chair, the female officer took notes.

Officer Vern sent Simone a text:

Sorry to wake you. Your instincts were correct. Jack was arrested. Found photos of him wearing your dress. Come to station at 9 to fill out paperwork.

Simone heard her phone ping, and bolted up in bed. She read the text. "Charlie, wake up," she said as she shook him. "Charlie . . . Charlie . . . they got him."

"What? What's wrong?" he said through a sleepy fog.

"The police arrested Jack. They found a photo of him wearing my dress."

"Really? That's great," he said yawning. "What time is it?"

"It's a little after four. I don't know about you, but I won't be able to go back to sleep," she said as she jumped out of bed. "Officer Vern said that I need to go to the station at nine to fill out some paperwork."

"Come back to bed and snuggle," Charlie mumbled. "You haven't had much sleep."

Simone thought about Charlie's tempting offer and acquiesced. She climbed back into bed, and snuggled up against him, spooning.

"Isn't that better?" he whispered, moments before she heard the gentle whistle of his breathing in her ear.

They awoke at seven-thirty, refreshed.

"I feel so much better knowing the police caught the person coming into my house," chirped Simone.

"I hate to burst your bubble, Simone, but you know, what Jack did might have been a one-time event. After all, you didn't meet Jack until after the first break-in, weeks ago, when your underwear was stolen. And I doubt he was the one sending you texts about Joe."

Simone's face dropped, her energy deflated in an instant. She sat down. "Oh, Charlie, I didn't think of that. I was so excited the police arrested Jack that I completely forgot about the other break-ins and texts. Do you think there's another person out there who's stalking me?"

"I'm afraid so, my love. Think about it. As I just mentioned, Jack was here after the first break-in."

Simone reflected on Charlie's analysis. "Remember he said he did work on this house years ago? Maybe he kept a key and was able to come in before I changed the locks. He could have stolen my underwear then. And after he changed the lock, maybe he kept a copy of the key, and left the roses. And the booties. Those were the same ones the intruder wore when the camera was placed in the lampshade. No, I disagree, Charlie. I think it was Jack who considered me easy prey."

Charlie questioned, "What are the chances that you would call him? Think about it, Simone."

"Well . . . that's a good point," she said reconsidering. "It could be that he knew Pete was on vacation, and that I would have to call the next local guy, who was he."

"That's really stretching it, Simone. You're assuming that Jack knows Pete, and knows he does all your work. "

"Pete did say he knows Jack."

"I think you want to convince yourself that Jack was the burglar."

"Okay. Let's say Jack saw me somewhere – the market, the beach – who knows. He followed me, and found out where I lived, which is only five minutes from his house. I had seen him in the area over the past few weeks."

Simone put down her mug and continued to speculate. "So, his first move was to break into my house. Remember last night I found my thong shoved in the corner of the drawer. He knew that I would call a locksmith, and he got a lucky break when I called him. He had offered to keep a copy of my key in his office, but I said no. Maybe he kept a copy anyway. Then, he came in and left the flowers. He knows my car, and could tell when I wasn't home. When he came by to plant the camera, he didn't see my car in the driveway or garage; he didn't know I had a loaner. He planted the camera and left. He also said that my back door could be opened with a credit card. Maybe I changed the lock for nothing. He always entered through the back door. The paper shoes convinced me. Remember, whoever came into my house wore those booties. And then, after installing the cameras, he came back again. It was Jack, I'm sure of it."

"But what about the text messages?" asked Charlie.

Twenty-Eight

Charlie decided he was going to accompany Simone to the police station, and afterward he'd go to work. "I want to hear what the police say about the other break-ins, and if they'd agree with your analysis. I'm not convinced."

They arrived at the Westport Police Station at nine o'clock, ready for Simone to sign papers. Hopefully, it would only take a few minutes.

"Thank you for coming down, Ms. Simpson. Charlie, it's good to see you again," said Officer Vern as the men shook hands. "I'm glad you're here with Simone, because some of the images we found in Jack's room are disturbing. Please, have a seat, and we'll go over everything."

The officer left the room while Charlie and Simone viewed over four dozen photos. There was Simone with Charlie on the beach, while she food shopped, in her car, on her phone, outside her office, and other familiar spots.

One photo piqued Charlie's interest. Simone was standing outside her front door, kissing Pete on the cheek. She giggled when she saw Charlie's frown. "Jealous?" she whispered.

"Please," he whispered back with a grin. "Have you seen my screwdriver?"

Simone blushed. The playful moment between the lovers was interrupted by the officer, followed by Police Chief Cindy Jacobs.

Chief Jacobs said, "Ms. Simpson, you're not the only person who had photos taken of them. Some of the other women are in much worse compromising situations. We're in the process of contacting the other victims. I fear that if we had not caught Mr. Miller last evening, and the interior camera had not been removed from your home, you may have become a victim to much worse.

"We will encourage the other women to press charges against him. And I am encouraging you to do the same."

The impact of it all hit Simone. *Press charges? Trials? Court time?* The silence suddenly was broken by a ping on Simone's phone.

"I'm sorry," she said. "Give me a second, and I'll shut off my phone."

She took a quick look at the text. The phone slipped out of her hand, landing on to the floor. Her throat caught as she mumbled, "Oh my God," followed by a sob.

Charlie picked up the phone and read the message:

Welcome home, Simone.
Did you think of me while making love? Joe

Police Chief Jacobs quickly moved around the desk, and took the phone from Charlie's hand. Her brown eyes, in need of reading glasses, squinted. Her face formed a look of disgust.

"I thought putting the cameras in your home, and arresting Jack would have taken care of this nonsense. Simone, I agree with Charlie, there's still someone out there stalking you. Do you have any idea who it could be?"

"No. Not at all," Simone said between tears. The list of possible intruders: Biff and Jack were quickly eliminated. Who else could it be?

The Chief continued. "The only thing we can do is wait for this person to make a mistake. Criminals often do. Just like Jack. He got sloppy. We can only hope this stalker makes a wrong move."

After further discussions about pressing charges, and endless forms requiring Simone's signature, she and Charlie left the station.

"I'll call you later. If it's busy at the hotel, and I don't get a chance to talk to you, I'll definitely see you tonight after class."

Simone kissed Charlie goodbye, got in her car, and headed up the Post Road towards her office. She stopped at Dunkin' Donuts drive- through in Southport, got an extra-large coffee, a dozen munch-kins, and continued on, feeling numb and distracted as she popped munchkin after munchkin in her mouth.

Who is the missing link? she wondered.

Twenty-Nine

"Simone, you don't look happy to be back. Didn't you and Charlie have a good time on your vacation?" Jennifer asked.

"We had a great time. Just problems at home. I had another break-in, even after the cameras were installed."

"Oh, no," Jennifer said as she sat down in Simone's office. "Did they capture the person on camera?"

"Yes, they did. And it was Jack, the locksmith perv. He put on one of my dresses, my makeup, and a necklace . . . who knows what else he did. I can't think about it." Simone could only imagine what more had transpired.

"Is he the one who stole your underwear, and is sending the text messages?"

Simone remained silent, feeling vulnerable. Someone was still out there sending her text messages. Could it be Jennifer? She hated thinking that, but she recalled all the times she received a text. Each and every time, Simone was alone, and Jennifer was someplace else. But why? She does like to get even . . .

"Simone, are you okay?" Jennifer asked, snapping her partner out of her daydreaming analysis.

"Jen, to be honest, I don't want to discuss it right now. It's only ten thirty in the morning and I'm already tired. Maybe work will distract me." She took in a deep breath and asked, "How was your flight home, and what's been happening while I was gone?"

Jennifer's demeanor went from concern for her business partner to animated giggles. "Simone, I met someone on the flight home. We talked the whole time, and we've been together ever since. I think I'm in love!" she exclaimed with excitement.

Simone tried her best to appear happy for Jennifer, and not roll her eyes. She knew how impulsive Jennifer was and how easily she fell in love. "Do I have to ask you the one hundred questions, or will you keep me in suspense?" Simone asked with a smile, playing along with her partner's new adventure.

"His name is Anthony. Don't call him Tony, he hates that name. Someone told him that mothers in Sicily wrote TO NY on their kid's foreheads, before sending them on a boat headed to the United States. Since then, he never wanted to be called Tony."

"I see," was all Simone could say. She pretended to be interested in Jennifer's latest drama, but she couldn't share in her friend's joy. *Why is this so torturous for me?* she wondered.

"Anthony lives in a cottage on the beach in Milford. It's so romantic, sitting outside at night with a fire pit burning, watching the sunset," Jennifer swooned. "He has a large Italian family, including a twin brother. I haven't met them yet, but I will - soon - I hope. I'm thinking of giving up my apartment, and moving in with him."

That last statement shocked Simone to attention. "Wow, that's a big move, don't you think?" Simone saw Jennifer's disappointment, and quickly added, "I mean, you really don't know him . . . you just met."

"I know, but I feel like I've met my soul mate, Simone. I really do."

Jennifer couldn't restrain her emotions. If only she was able to step back and take things slowly, she wouldn't have gone through two quick marriages, and a dangerous night with a killer. Simone countered, "Jennifer, I'm anxious to get back to work. Maybe we can catch up later this afternoon, after I return these phone calls," she said, holding up a handful of phone message slips.

"Sure . . . later . . . after lunch," Jennifer said, with obvious annoyance.

"I'm sorry, Jennifer. I've got a lot on my mind. I got back from Europe last night. I'm jet lagged, and spent this morning at the Westport police station filling out forms, looking at photographs . . ."

But Simone never got to finish her sentence. "I understand," Jennifer mumbled as she stood up. "I'm sorry to have shoved my personal life on you. I know how you prefer we keep our private lives separate."

There was that jab again, but Simone held her temper. "Jennifer," was all she said as her partner closed the door behind her.

I don't have time for her drama, Simone mused.

She opened her laptop, and wiggled the mouse to wake up the machine. She logged in, and saw she had forty-five unanswered e-mails. "The punishment for taking a vacation," she said out loud.

She picked up her stack of phone messages. There were three from Judy Smith, her college roommate. Simone immediately called her back.

"Judy," I'm so happy to hear from you. I just got back from Europe last night. I'm sorry it took me so long to get in touch. How are you? How are your parents?"

"Well, that's what I'm calling about, Simone," Judy said with deep sadness in her voice. "Simone, my dad passed away from a massive heart attack. His funeral was yesterday."

"Oh, no. That can't be, Judy," Simone cried into the phone. "No, I don't believe what you're saying. I just spoke to him the day before I left for Paris. What happened? Was your mom with him?"

"No. He was in court, and just fell over, and died."

"Judy, I'll be there by this evening. I have to go home and pack a few things." Through tears, Simone stuttered, "Judy, my heart is broken. Please, tell your mom I'm coming."

"Thank you, Simone. Your room will be ready. My mom and I need your support. I love you."

"I love you, too, my friend," she said.

Simone got on line and booked a flight to Charlottesville, Virginia for later that afternoon. She sat in her chair and sobbed as she never had before. All the pain she had been keeping at bay spewed forth. She cried for the loss of Mr. Smith, a wonderful man, whom, along with his wife, helped Simone through one of the most difficult times in her life. Mr. Smith 'gave her away' when she married Joe, and she lived with the family after Joe's death. Added to that, the stress from recent events: the break-ins, Biff's murder, Jack, the text messages, her annoyance with Jennifer . . . and now, the passing of the man she loved like a father. It all came to a boil as her tears flowed. Her sobs reverberated throughout the office.

"Should we go see if she's alright?" Katy asked Jennifer.

"No, leave her alone," Jennifer said as she held Katy back from entering Simone's office. "I think there's more going on with her than we know."

Deep down, Jennifer didn't care what was going on with Simone at the moment. She deserves it, Jennifer thought. Just as quickly, she chided herself for the anger toward Simone for not wanting to know about Anthony. She knew she wasn't being fair to her partner. But Simone's rule about not involving each other with their private lives became too complicated at times.

Simone reprimanded herself for losing control in the office. After all, she was the Queen of Control when things went wrong. She wiped away her tears, blew her nose and did a quick to-do list in her mind. She shoved her laptop, phone messages, and files into her messenger bag, opened her office door, and, as she headed toward the exit shouted, "I have a family emergency. I'll be gone for the rest of the week. Text me if you need me." The staff watched from the window as Simone got into her car and sped away.

"Family?" murmured Jennifer to no one in particular. She turned to Katy and asked to see the carbon copies of Simone's messages. Three calls from Judy Smith. I bet something happened to her parents. Jennifer regretted acting so bubbly, going on about Anthony when Simone was dealing with her own issues.

She texted her:

Whatever is going on, know that I'm here for you. Jen

But Simone never responded. She drove to her house, quickly threw some clothes into a suitcase, and headed to Westchester Airport for her flight. She needed to be with her soul sister and best friend, Judy, and her adopted mother, Virginia.

At the airport, she texted Charlie and told him Mr. Smith died, and she was headed to be with the family.

He texted back:

I'm sorry to hear about Mr. Smith. Let me know if you want me to join you. Extend my sympathies to Judy and Mrs. Smith. Love you.

Sudden deaths surrounded her: her parents, Joe, their unborn baby, Casey Bouvier, Biff, and now, Mr. Smith.

And Charlie wonders why I fear he will die too.

Thirty

"Hi Judy, its Jennifer Keys. Simone left the office saying she had a family emergency. Is everything okay at your home?"

"Thank you for calling, Jennifer. My dad died last week, and he was buried yesterday. I know how much Simone loved him. My dad considered her a daughter."

"Oh, I'm sorry, Judy. Please extend my condolences to your mother and family. Is there anything we can do back here in Connecticut?"

"I don't think so, but thank you for checking in. I'll tell my mother you send your condolences."

Jennifer disconnected, and told Katy and Jonathan that Simone's college friend's father had died. They were very close. "In fact, after Simone's husband was killed, the Smith family took Simone in, and she lived with them for a few years."

"Her husband was killed?" asked Katy. "I didn't know that. How awful for her," she added.

"I'm not sure Simone really wants anyone to know how her husband died. And I probably should not have said anything to you two, so please keep it to yourself."

"Her secret is safe with me," Jonathan said.

Kathy mimed locking her lips, and throwing away the key.

Jennifer looked through the rest of the phone messages, and returned calls for Simone, explaining that she had to leave the office for a few days. Was there anything she could do to help?

There were calls from people Simone had met at a recent Chamber of Commerce after-hours event. One wanted to speak to Simone about a Bar Mitzvah for her son. Jennifer made an appointment with the woman, planning to bring Jonathan with her. He had a lot of patience with teens. He had stopped more than a few food fights from getting out of control.

Another was a nine-year old's birthday party. Jennifer handed that information on to Katy.

Jennifer concluded that if she and Simone were going to move Jonathan and Katy up to full time planners, now would be a good time to test their abilities.

"You know, Katy, I often made fun of Simone for keeping this old-fashioned carbon copy telephone book. But it makes a lot of sense. 'Don't fix it if it ain't broke.'"

Jennifer created new folders for the clients, taped the phone messages inside the related folders, and sent Simone another text:

> *Returned calls from Chamber people. Under control. No need for you to call them. Take care of yourself. Jennifer*

> *What referrals from the Chamber event?* Simone texted back.

"Oops," Jennifer said out loud. She replied:

> *I spoke to Judy. Very sorry about her dad.*
> *Called Jacobs-Bar Mitzvah. Taking Jonathan to meeting.*
> *Cunningham- 9 year old party. Gave to Katy.*

Simone texted back, her temper rising:

> *Did I ask you to make these calls?*

Jennifer stared at her phone with surprise. She could tell that Simone was angry. Why can't I make decisions? After all, I'm a partner in this firm, Jennifer wondered.

Over the loudspeaker, the pilot announced: "Ladies and gentlemen, please turn off all cell phones and other electronic devices. We will be taxiing in a few minutes."

Jennifer texted Simone again:

> *I'm sorry. I thought I was helping,*

But Simone's phone went silent.

Thirty-One

Before leaving for the day, Jennifer went online, and ordered a large fruit basket to be delivered to the Smith home. She hoped Simone wouldn't be angry about that, too.

I'm just trying to be helpful, she kept telling herself. *There's no satisfying Simone. Everything has to be done her way. She has to call the clients, and makes all the decisions. Well, I can make decisions, too.* Jennifer's defenses increased as she drove to Milford, and on to Anthony's cottage.

Goober, Anthony's rescue dog greeted her with barking, jumping and wet kisses. He was a mutt, with the slobbering of a St. Bernard, the body of a Shephard, and the love of a Labrador. His tail had enough strength to knock over a small child. He loved running out the back door of Anthony's cottage, down the flight of concrete steps, and charging into the waters of Long Island Sound.

Goober shed enough to create a fur-companion. He smelled. Anthony's cottage smelled. Anthony's car smelled. Everywhere Goober went, he left his aroma. But Anthony smelled heavenly of musk and Irish Spring soap.

When Anthony and Jennifer were having sex, Goober had to be locked out of the bedroom. Otherwise, he'd jump on the bed, and wedge his smelly body between them. Once, he growled at Jennifer when Anthony cried out of pleasure.

Most evenings after dinner, Jennifer, Anthony and Goober took a walk along the beach, tossing a stick or tennis ball for the dog. He'd splash in the water, the temperature not bothering his thick coat, retrieved the item and dropped it for another round of fetch. He loved shaking his body and drenching the couple.

That evening, over dinner, Jennifer told Anthony about Simone's reaction to her taking the initiative to run the office.

"Hey, babe, don't worry about her. She sounds like a stuck-up bitch. Why don't you dump her, and go out on your own? You'll run circles around her," Anthony encouraged.

"No, I can't do that. Simone's been good to me. I think she has lots of things going on in her life, and she's stressed."

"You're making excuses for her. I'd quit if my boss treated me that way."

"I can't leave. I'm committed," Jennifer said.

Anthony pushed the issue. "Why not? No one owns you."

"Because, I'm a partner in the firm. I can't just walk out."

Anthony's brown eyes widened at this news. "A partner, huh?" He paused and ran his fingers through his perfectly coiffed hair. She tried to read his reaction, but his face was expressionless. "From what you tell me, Simone must be doing well: fancy car, trips to Europe, a nice house. She should be grateful she has you to step in and take charge."

"It sounds glamorous, but it really isn't. She's had her share of troubles. I can't go out on my own without hiring an attorney to break the contract. Besides, I could never be a planner in the same town."

"So, come up to Milford, or another town north of Fairfield, and open your own place," he countered. "Anywhere away from her. There's Guilford, Madison, and New Haven. Maybe you can get a job at Yale, or at a corporation in Hartford. You won't need to rent an office, and maybe you'll get benefits. Businesses are always doing conferences and meetings. You'd be a natural. And you can work on the side handling private events and weddings. Anybody else in the office not happy with Simone? Maybe they'll join you."

"The only one would be Jonathan, but I don't think he's unhappy. He might move because he's single, and I don't think he has any family ties."

"Is he good looking?" Anthony teased.

"Yes, very. Tall, lean Latin. The women love him," she countered.

"Whoa, babe," Anthony said. "You think I'd let you go into business with a single, good looking dude?" He chuckled. "I'm the only good looking one you're ever going to be with."

Jennifer laughed, but she knew he was serious. "He's gay," she responded quickly. "No worries there."

"Okay. I just don't want anyone taking my baby away from me," he said. He reached over the table and gave her a deep kiss that stirred an arousal.

He sat back down. "Think about it. Any money you make will be all yours. You won't have to share it with Simone."

Anthony fueled Jennifer's impulsive instincts.

"It sounds tempting," she said." But where would I get the equity to start my own company? It takes money to open an office . . . rent, office furniture, phones, web designers, computers, utilities, staff . . . ." her words trailed off. *Although, it would be nice to have my own business,* she thought.

"How do you know Simone isn't playing with the books, and isn't giving you a fair share?"

His words were sobering.

"I don't think Simone would cheat me, Anthony. She's not like that. Although, I have been thinking that she seems to have lots of money available to her. She bought the house by the beach . . . I was with her . . . and she sank a ton of money to fix it up, and had it professionally decorated. She drives a Porsche. I bet she's got a nice nest egg tucked away that I don't know about."

"Babe, money or no money, she shouldn't have scolded you for doing your job. She's your boss, not your mother."

He paused a moment, contemplating his next move. His eyes shifted, then back at Jennifer to read her face. "I assume you must have a nice nest egg, too, by now. You're always working, and the company does well. Between your salary and a percentage of the company's profits, I'd think you've got some solid money by now."

Jennifer didn't show a reaction – a poker face – taught to her by Simone. It was important to be nonplused when working with difficult and demanding clients. She thought it was a little pushy of Anthony to ask about her finances, especially since they'd only been dating for a few weeks. She convinced herself he was simply helping her think through her options.

"Well, I do have some money socked away for retirement." She paused, then said, "Unfortunately, I spend a lot on my shoes, clothes and jewelry." Hearing the words out loud made her feel foolish and reckless.

"Retirement is years away, babe. I think you should quit your job and use that money to make a fresh start."

"Maybe you're right," Jennifer mused.

"You know I am," he said.

"I'll think about it. Maybe it is time for me to go out on my own. Anthony, you're the best. Thank you for talking this over with me. I didn't see it the way you do."

"Anything for you, babe. Now, let's frustrate Goober and lock the bedroom door."

Thirty-Two

Simone sat at the Philadelphia airport terminal, waiting for the connecting flight to Charlottesville. It was delayed because of storms, adding to her anxiety. *When you need to get someplace in a hurry, there always seems to be delays,* she muttered to herself. In Charlottesville, she'll rent a car and drive the hour to the Smith's home, hoping to be there no later than seven o'clock.

During her initial flight, Simone reflected back on the tragedies in her life. After leaving Louisville to go to NYU, her father had disowned her for not obeying his demands. He claimed he wanted her to go to a local college, live at home, and care for her parents in their declining years. They were healthy, and only in their early fifties. No, her father didn't want her to care for them, he wanted her there so she could become like her mother, a victim of his physical, sexual and emotional abuse, especially after one of his drinking binges.

Simone's mother chided her for telling a "false story" after her father had raped her when she was twelve. After that, Simone slept with a baseball bat in her bed, determined to use it if her father ever came near her again. He made sure she was aware of his physical attraction to her, something that turned Simone's stomach every time she thought about it.

The only way she knew how to get away from him, was to apply to a college out of state. She was accepted with scholarships to New York University. Once she told her parents she had accepted the offer, her father forbid her to communicate with them, or to return home.

She wrote to her parents every week, included photographs of her and her roommate, Judy. None of her letters were answered. Once she called and briefly spoke to her mother, before her father grabbed the phone and terminated the conversation. Her mother probably received a beating for saying hello to her daughter.

After a year of abandonment, her mother sent Simone a letter via a neighbor. For months, they communicated in secret. Days before a secret planned meeting in Philadelphia, her parents were killed in a car accident. Her father was driving drunk, crashed head on into a tree, and they were killed instantly.

Then, years later, she and Joe were walking to their favorite restaurant, when Simone would tell him he was going to be a father. He was killed by a speeding taxi before she could share the good news.

And now, after a glorious vacation with Charlie, feeling more in love with him than ever, Mr. Smith died. It seems whenever she was on a 'high' in life, something came along to destroy her happiness. She wondered if Charlie would ever understand her fears of losing him, too.

She was feeling sorry for herself. *Well-deserved*, she thought.

She sat on the hard yellow plastic seat in the security area, her right leg rapidly twitching up and down with nervous energy, symbolically crushing the bad memories. She was angry - with everyone and everything – including herself. Why was she afraid of her relationship with Charlie? If he lived with her or not, she would feel the same pain if he died. He wasn't sick, so why did she think he was going to die? The reason was obvious.

She wondered why she was angry with Jennifer for taking charge. Isn't that what a business partner is supposed to do? She now regretted the words she texted her, reprimanding her for making the business calls in her absence. The fact was, Simone wouldn't have time to return calls for several more days. All the nonsense about Jack disgusted her . . . the photos, the criminal charges, and the possibly of a court case. But they were defenses, and she owed Jennifer an apology.

Simone's flight was suddenly announced. She gathered her suitcase and started walking toward the gate. She wanted to check her phone for missed calls before having to shut it off again on the plane. She pulled her phone out of her purse. A text had come in:

There's no pain where I am. Join me.
Forever yours, Joe.

Thirty-Three

Upon hearing the crunching of the gravel in the driveway, Judy ran to the front door.

"Simone," she cried, as the two women fell into each other's arms. Tears, hugs and words of comfort were exchanged.

"Judy," Simone said, "I'm sorry I wasn't here last week. I only wish someone in the office had contacted me. I would have come home sooner."

"I spoke with Katy in your office. She told me you and Charlie were on vacation in Nice. I told her not to contact you. There was nothing you could have done to change what happened. Nothing would bring back my father . . ." Judy's words trailed off as new tears poured forth.

Irene, the Smith's housekeeper, a boxy woman of Russian descent, came out from the house. "Oh Miss Simone, you little thing," she said, as she hugged her. "Thank you for coming to comfort the Missus, and Miss Judy."

She lowered her voice to a whisper so only Simone could hear, "It was awful, Miss Simone. I'm afraid the shock will make Mrs. Smith ill if she's not careful. Please watch over her, and make her eat something. She's becoming skin and bones, the poor thing. She'll listen to you."

"I'll do my best, Irene," Simone whispered back the promise.

"Let me get your bags and put them in your bedroom," Irene said with renewed energy.

Virginia Smith, Judy's mother, came out onto the porch, the wooden screen door slamming behind her. She wiped her hands on her white and yellow-flowered apron before bringing Simone into her embrace.

As Mrs. Smith reminisced about how she and Henry met, Simone devoured a deep bowl of beef stew and vegetables, her favorite comfort food. She washed down the meal with two large glasses of lemony iced tea. She was famished, realizing the last time she ate was before she and Charlie went to the police station that morning.

"Mrs. Smith, I don't know what to say, other than I feel like I've just lost my father. When my own father died, I had no remorse, no feelings towards him. He was an abusive man . . ." Her words faded as she dismissed the memory of him.

The women chatted as Irene prepared the next morning's breakfast: she mixed eggs, milk, mustard, cheese, and cooked sausage in a bowl. She poured the contents into a large buttered Pyrex dish, covered it with aluminum foil, and placed it in the refrigerator. Then she measured out the ingredients for Simone's favorite: Irene's homemade biscuits.

"Tomorrow's breakfast is prepared," Irene said with a satisfied smile. Turning to Mrs. Smith, "Missus, if you don't need me . . ."

"Irene, thank you. Yes, you can retire for the evening."

"I'll be here bright and early to prepare Miss Simone's favorite breakfast."

Simone got up and gave Irene a hug. "Thank you for taking care of me, and for being here for Mrs. Smith and Judy. You're a godsend."

Simone begged for a cup of strong coffee. "I have a lot of work to do tonight. I'm afraid I'll be up past midnight."

Judy acquiesced, handing over the creamer.

"You remembered," Simone smiled.

"Someone brought over a homemade apple pie," Judy said removing it from the refrigerator. Simone's face lit up. She nodded her head approvingly. "Just a small piece."

As Simone ate a second piece of pie, she told the women about Charlie, his difficulties with his disapproving father, his money-hungry soon-to-be ex-wife, and how his nephew, Frederick, planted listening devices in their rooms. And she regaled about Barbara and Biff, and how he had attacked her, and how later that night he was murdered.

Conversation turned to Judy's work as a special-needs teacher in Richmond and her life in that big city. She was dating Harold, a chemistry teacher whom she met at a conference a year ago. Judy spoke,

"I'm so sorry, Mrs. Smith," Simone said with renewed tears. "He was a wonderful man . . . more like a father to me . . . I will miss him so much . . ." she consoled.

"Thank you for coming, Simone," Mrs. Smith managed to mutter. "Come inside. I'm sure Irene can put something together for you to eat."

The two women walked into the house arm in arm, with Judy close behind. Memories of happier times ran through Simone's mind. The first time she came to this house she was a freshman in college. She had nowhere to go during spring break, and Judy brought her suitemate with her to the hills of Virginia. Many meals were shared at the large Chippendale style table, always set for the next meal of the day. Mr. Smith sat at the head of the table, as if holding court, and he would say grace before every meal.

Although the Smith's were a religious family, they never forced their beliefs on Simone, nor did they insist she attend church on Sunday. She was always invited to join them, and, sometimes she did. But her religious beliefs were tentative, to say the least. She saw, and experienced, too much pain and suffering to believe there was a just God.

Year after year, Simone and Judy came home during their summer breaks to work at the local country club, and enjoy lazy days sitting on the porch, listening to Mr. Smith read aloud from one of his law books, while Mrs. Smith crocheted. Surprisingly, no one ever got bored listening to the details of past court cases. Simone often found them fascinating. They'd watch twinkling fireflies, and listen to the fluttering moths as they gathered around the porch light, as if having a family gathering of their own.

Simone and Judy, free of doing homework or racing to classes, would sit and rock in the twin, white rattan rockers while sipping iced teas served in sweating tumblers.

Now, the three women sat around the kitchen table, with Virginia recapping the story of how her husband, Henry, died while defending a wrongly accused teen of murder.

"He just keeled over. That was it. At least he didn't suffer, thank the Lord."

enthusiastically, as she described the new man in her life. "He's arriving tomorrow, Simone. I can't wait for you meet him."

"He's a true southern gentleman," Virginia added. "His father is also an attorney, and he and Henry often went to battle in the courtroom. The world is so small." Her eyes filmed when she mentioned her husband's name. Brushing away a tear, she asked, "Are you happy, Simone?"

Simone's face morphed from a smile to a sob. She looked at Judy, and then at Mrs. Smith, and three seconds later cried, "I'm in trouble," she said. "I'm in deep trouble."

Thirty-Four

Simone described the events that had taken place over the past months, starting with the first text message to the one she received that day between flights.

"Do you have any idea who would be so cruel?" asked Mrs. Smith.

"No, I don't." Simone hesitated, putting her thoughts aside.

Feeling guilty, she added, "I'm sorry Mrs. Smith. You just buried your husband, and here I am telling you about my troubles. I'm being selfish. I apologize."

"Simone, no need to stop. Life is for the living. You're family. We should be able to talk about our respective lives, especially when someone is trying to destroy it."

"Destroy it . . . yes, that's it . . . someone is trying to destroy my life. I didn't think of it that way. At first, I found it more of an annoyance, and I've been so busy with work that I haven't focused on the reality of the situation. Charlie questioned if there was another man, and we had a big fight because I kept information from him for months."

"Try not to do that, my dear," interrupted Mrs. Smith. "Don't keep secrets from your man. It's not good for the relationship," she said with maternal authority. "After a while, he'll want to know what else you are keeping from him."

Simone was reminded of the baby she had lost. She stopped speaking and stared past the women, the hurt of losing her husband and baby flooding back.

"You still miss him, don't you?" Virginia asked.

Simone knew who she was talking about. Refocusing, she answered, "Yes." Fresh tears sprang forth.

"Joe is no longer here, Simone. And you're punishing Charlie for that. Charlie sounds like a wonderful man. You're blessed to have had two good men come your way."

"Mrs. Smith, you always know what to say. Thank you."

"It comes with age, my dear," she said stroking Simone's hair. "Just have someone to grow old with," Virginia said, as the two women cried together.

Virginia, Judy and Simone stayed up until past midnight, listening to Simone's stories about the text messages, the break-ins, Jack's arrest, and the imminent trial.

"I know if Henry was here, he'd be the first one to help you."

"Yes . . . yes, he would," Simone said.

"Before we become three weeping willows, let's get some sleep," suggested Mrs. Smith. "I expect to see you two down here by seven thirty."

"Yes, ma'am," the two women responded.

Mrs. Smith ran a tight household, and never tolerated people sleeping past seven o'clock, unless sick in bed. "You're letting the world pass you by," she would add. "You can sleep when your toes are pointing up to God."

The next morning, Simone awoke to the heavenly smells of luscious custard, freshly baked flaky biscuits and coffee brewed with a sprig of chicory. She quickly showered, dressed, and was sitting at the breakfast table in less than twenty minutes.

"Irene, you're wonderful," Simone cooed. "Can I steal you, and bring you back to Connecticut?"

"Do you have chickens where I can get my fresh eggs?"

"No, but some neighbors have constructed coops, so we can steal eggs every morning," Simone teased.

"What about cows for fresh milk, pigs for fresh sausage, and a vegetable garden in your back yard. Look out the window, Miss Simone. All of that is available here."

"I surrender, Irene. You've got me beat. I don't have room for any farm animals or a garden. In fact, I don't even have plants because I'm never home. My housekeeper occasionally brings me a succulent plant, but that too, I manage to kill. It seems the only green I touch is money."

"Irene chuckled," privy to Simone's personal finances. "You city girls need to get your hands dirty. Feel the earth, talk to her, and she'll talk back."

"You mean like Scarlett O'Hara's Tara?"

The elderly woman's head titled back and, as she laughed, a few white hairs escaped from their confinement in a bun.

"What are you two laughing about?" Mrs. Smith asked, as she joined them in the kitchen."

"Irene was giving me some life lessons on how to milk a cow and steal eggs from chickens," Simone said jokingly. "And something about <u>Gone with the Wind</u>."

"Oh Miss Simone," said Irene, "If I were going to teach you anything about that movie, it would be to find a good man, and never let him go."

Suddenly, there was an uncomfortable silence in the room.

Knowing Irene didn't mean any harm by the comment, Simone said, "Oh, I thought you were going to give me sewing lessons on how to make a dress from draperies."

"I can hear your laughter from all the way upstairs," announced Judy, as she entered the kitchen. "I hope there was time to prepare breakfast in between these comedy acts."

"Sit down, child," Irene said to Judy. "You know in my kitchen, there's always something to eat."

Although the uncomfortable moment passed, there was still a sense of loss permeating in the room.

After breakfast, Mrs. Smith, Judy and Simone sat on the veranda, watching the shadows of daylight dancing in the distance. They sat in the old, white wicker rockers. On a side table was a pitcher of iced tea with lemon slices and sprigs of mint from Irene's garden. Condensation dripped down the jug onto an absorbent linen towel, featuring colorful hand embroidery.

Remembering what Charlie had said about her home: *"I wish I could sit here all day, every day. This is so peaceful."* Simone felt the same about the Smith's home. "I've missed this so much. My house overlooks the ocean. Here, it's hills and farms. I don't know which I love more."

"You can love them both." Virginia said.

Simone smiled, understanding the unspoken message.

The women sat silently, rocking slowly, enjoying these last moments of sunrise. Each day, the morning air brought a hint of pending autumn.

"Simone, I need to talk to you about something," Mrs. Smith announced, breaking the peaceful post-breakfast dozing.

Virginia reached into the pocket of her apron, and pulled out an envelope. "Years ago, when Mr. Smith drew up his will, he and I discussed the distribution of his estate." Her announcement broke the tranquil ambiance. "Of course, the house and farm, and all of his possessions are left to me, as well as provisions for Judy."

Simone quickly looked at Judy, who only smiled. Simone was convinced that Judy knew where this conversation was headed. She was always a step or two ahead of Simone. She knew hours before that Joe was going to propose that evening, and now, Judy knew what was coming.

Simone stopped rocking, focusing on Mrs. Smith's voice.

She continued, "Henry loved you very much, Simone."

Simone nodded, a fact she never questioned. Mrs. Smith's words brought fresh tears, enhancing Simone's green eyes, and making her throat feel thick.

"We had discussed this at length, and revisited his decision when we updated our wills two years ago. He left you this letter to read upon his death. Of course, it hasn't yet gone through probate, but I doubt anyone would object to his wishes."

She handed the envelope to Simone, then added, "Since we don't see you often, Judy and I thought it best to give this to you now, in person."

She and Judy sat back and watched as Simone opened the envelope, her hands shaking slightly.

Dearest Simone,

If you're reading this, you know the outcome of my demise. Don't cry, child. I'm with my Lord, and I am happy.

I have instructed my wife, my daughter, and my attorney to fulfil my last wishes. And I am asking you to do the same. If my wife or daughter predecease me, please be sure my final requests are satisfied.

During World War II, I was a young soldier stationed in France. Although Paris wasn't bombed as badly as other cities, people fled out of fear, abandoning their homes and businesses.

One day, on a three-day furlough, I went to Paris, and walked among the uninhabited homes. Although things looked grim, I still fell in love with the City, and with Marguerite, an 80 year old woman. We met while she watered a single flower in front of the building where she lived. "I have faith," she said to me in French.

She invited me to her apartment, where she prepared a simple lunch from her rations. She told me her husband died in World War I, leaving her with two small boys. In 1943, both boys died as a result of the current war. She had no one.

Being in the Army, I did not know when I could return to visit her. I volunteered for any assignment that would bring me back to Paris and Marguerite. I missed my family, especially my mother, and Marguerite was the closest person to making me feel I was home.

I visited her four additional times over the next nine months, each time leaving with a full belly, and a broken heart for the troubles she had in her life. No one should suffer as she did.

Then, I was transferred to Germany, and my visits to Marguerite ended. When I got a one-week furlough, I hitched a ride with some buddies, and returned to Paris. I discovered Marguerite had died five months before. A neighbor asked if I was "The" Henry Smith Marguerite had talked about. I showed her my dog tags as proof. She brought me to her apartment, which was next door to Marguerite's, and said her neighbor had left something for me.

She handed me an envelope, as I do to you, today. Inside was a letter, leaving me all her possessions, including her five bedroom apartment. She called me her adopted son, her closest family member.

As of the writing of this will, I am still the owner of the apartment. The building turned "condo" so to speak in the 1990s, and I have the deed, which I pass on to you.

Marguerite took me in as her son, and left me her prized possession. Virginia and I took you in so many years ago, and considered you our adopted daughter. I, like Marguerite, would like to leave you my prized possession, a penthouse apartment on Rue des Barres in Paris.

It is the same apartment you and Judy stayed the summer of your senior year. I told you it belonged to a fellow attorney in my office, but it really belonged to me.

In addition to the deed to this apartment, I've instructed my attorneys to set up a trust fund with $250,000 for the upkeep and maintenance of the property.

Enjoy the apartment any way you see fit, as a getaway, as a future home, or as a place you'll find solace to contemplate life.

With my eternal love for you, my adopted daughter,

Henry Smith

"Mrs. Smith, Judy, I cannot accept this. This is too much. I'm lost for words," wept Simone.

Judy responded. "Simone, my father was a very astute business man, and knew a good thing when he saw it. Not only did he purchase Marguerite's apartment, he also purchased the neighbor's apartment. He paid above asking price, and made arrangements for her to live there, rent free, for the rest of her life.

"She died eight years ago, and the apartment has been my father's ever since. Now, upon his death, he left the apartment to me. How do you do, neighbor?"

The two women hugged, laughed and cried.

Mrs. Smith asked that the three of them join hands, and say a prayer in remembrance of Henry Smith, a smart and most generous man whose memory would live on.

Thirty-Five

Simone's visit to Charlottesville lasted five days, too short to completely relax and catch up with her "family", and too long being away from her office, and Charlie. She was still in blissful shock over the inheritance of the Paris apartment, and couldn't wait to tell Charlie.

Simone needed to get back to the office, to catch up on past due responsibilities, and make amends with Jennifer. She called the office four times in the past three days, but Jennifer was never available, nor did she respond to texts. Either she told the office staff to say she wasn't in, or she was playing hooky. Simone suspected she was getting even, and took a holiday, spending time at Anthony's cottage.

Finally, on Simone's last call to the office on Friday afternoon, Jennifer picked up. She sounded reserved and curt.

"Hi Jennifer, how are you. I called a few times. How are things in the office?"

"Fine." she said, never asking Simone how things were at the Smith home, or why she didn't return her boss' calls.

Uncomfortable silence followed.

"O-kay . . . ." Simone said, emphasizing the word. "Please ask Jonathan to prepare the final invoice for the Bradshaw wedding. Be sure he includes all the purchases we made on Barbara Kemp's behalf, including travel expenses, and the rest."

"I'll tell him."

"I'll be back in the office on Monday."

"Okay," Jennifer said.

Simone paused for a long, awkward moment, and then added, "Jennifer, if you wish to play this game, play it by yourself. I will not have a business partner with an attitude. I don't appreciate your need to get even with me if I say or do something that upsets you. I know I was out of line for snapping at you about returning phone calls, and I apologize. I was in the middle of a very stressful situation, and should have appreciated you taking charge."

Jennifer did not say a word, but let silence fill the air.

Simone continued, "Apparently, you're not happy with the way I run the business. If you're unhappy, you can make a change. I'll be back in town tomorrow evening. I hope to see you in the office on Monday after you've had time to think about our conversation. If you feel you want to behave in the same manner, I'll be sorry to see you go."

"Simone . . ."

But Simone had hung up.

Thirty-Six

A tropical depression hugged the Atlantic coast, which caused flight delays and cancellations. Simone's flight was delayed four hours, getting her into Westchester Airport at nine p.m. An Uber driver was waiting for her as she left the main terminal.

The drive back to Westport was equally delayed with bumper to bumper traffic on the Merritt Parkway.

"It's been like this since four o'clock this afternoon," the driver said. "A tractor trailer jackknifed in Bridgeport. It tipped over and landed on top of two cars. One of the cars was flattened, killing two people, and three in the second car also died. Everywhere you go, there's traffic."

"That's horrible," Simone said from the back seat.

Simone yearned for the quiet, peaceful roads in Charlottesville. Connecticut highways were becoming racing tracks, with drivers weaving in and out and tailgating. There was an increase in rear-end collisions from people who were texting while driving, and not paying attention to the road ahead.

As a result of the deadly accident, cars were forced off the major interstate and onto the small, two-lane country highway. Tractor trailers were restricted from the Merritt Parkway, forcing them to drive on the Post Road.

"Did you have a nice flight, Miss?" the driver asked, trying to make conversation. But Simone was tired, and in no mood to discuss her day.

"If it's okay with you, I'd like to get some work done," she said, trying to be polite, while implying she didn't want to talk.

Normally, the drive from Westchester Airport to her home took thirty-five minutes. They were an hour into the drive, and still had twenty more miles to go. At this pace, it would be at least another hour before they reached Westport.

She thought about her home, and wondered what surprises would face her when she got there. Pete had once again changed the lock - actually, all the locks -- this time to a Smart Lock, opened by using her cell phone. And as a precaution, he also installed a deadbolt lock. She asked Pete to replace her back door with a solid steel one, and to install matching locks.

It seemed she was dealing with overlapping intruders. Jack, for sure, as the police found proof of him inside her house. She suspected he was in her house while she had hidden under her bed. One was the underwear stealer, the second, the one sending her the texts. But she could be wrong, and it's been Jack all along. *Wouldn't that be nice*, she thought, as she closed her eyes for only a second.

She felt someone shaking her. "Miss . . . Miss . . . wake up," the driver said. "You're home."

Simone opened her eyes, and for a split second, didn't know where she was. "Oh, I'm sorry,"

"That's okay, Miss. It happens all the time. I'll help you with your luggage."

The driver opened the quiet gate, which made Simone smile. As she put her foot on the first step, motion lights went on, lighting her way up to her front door. This brought a grin to her face, and a silent thank you to Pete.

She found the app on her phone, scanned it against the smart lock, and she heard the metal bolt unlock. She inserted her house key into the deadbolt lock, and heard the second metal bolt move. She turned the knob and opened her front door.

She handed the driver a generous tip, and said good night. She turned on the lights, and did a thorough inspection. Her clothes were in their correct order, no flower deliveries, and no cameras. No one had been there, not even Anna Maria.

Her phone pinged. She hoped it was Charlie, who was working that evening. He told her he would try to get away before the wedding cake was served, and would be at her place before midnight. It was already close to that time. She remembered the traffic on the Merritt Parkway, and was sure Charlie had changed his mind.

She read the text:

> *"Hello love. I hope you had a good flight.*
> *I'll be at your place tomorrow in time for brunch.*
> *Tonight's wedding is keeping me here. Charlie*

She texted back:

> *Just got home. Exhausted. Everything is fine.*
> *See you tomorrow. Love you.*

The next morning, she arose at six, showered, dressed, and went for a long walk along the beach. As the fall air nipped at her face and fingers, she was happy she wore a sweatshirt. She heard her phone ping again, and assumed it was Charlie saying good morning. She stopped walking and slipped the phone out of her back pocket.

The text read:

> *Welcome home. With all my love, Joe*

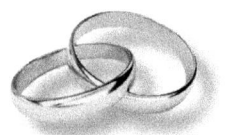

Thirty-Seven

When Simone returned to the office on Monday, she didn't know what to expect. What she found was an empty office void of employees. *That's strange,* she thought. As she walked through the office, she flipped on the lights. In the kitchen she prepared a cappuccino. She returned to her desk and started reviewing e-mails.

Within fifteen minutes, Jennifer arrived. Simone looked up from her laptop, saw it was Jennifer, and lowered her eyes quickly. She was determined not to give in. Jennifer needed to apologize, and inform Simone if she was going to stay on as her partner, or leave. Simone needed to apologize as well. Was this going to be a battle of "who blinks first?"

"Hi," Jennifer said as she stood at the threshold of Simone's office door. "How is Mrs. Smith?"

"She's devastated. Mr. Smith was her world. She sends her thanks for the fruit basket. That was very thoughtful of you."

"I'm glad."

Silence. Simone felt as if she was about to enter into a sword fight. She wondered who was going to respond first. She stopped typing, and looked up at Jennifer.

"So," Jennifer said, "I thought about what you said . . . about my attitude."

Simone kept her face expressionless. The poker face she mastered, and taught to Jennifer and her other staff. Jennifer and Jonathan were equally masterful, but Katy struggled keeping her emotions in check. Simone enjoyed watching Jennifer squirm. She knew she wasn't being nice, but she didn't care.

"It seems I don't get to make any of the major decisions regarding the clients," Jennifer continued.

"When have I kept you out of the loop of any of the decisions? Can you give me an example?"

"Well, when I told you about the two calls from Chamber members. You texted, 'did I ask you to call them?' I took care of the two calls, and we have the contracts for a little girl's birthday party, and a Bar Mitzvah. Both have substantial budgets."

"That's great, Jennifer. I'm happy we got signed contracts for both of them. But I met those people at Chamber meetings. I built up the relationship with them over several months. I didn't think it was appropriate for them to hear from a complete stranger, because I was too busy. Another few hours of waiting to get back to them, would not have killed the deals."

Simone continued, "But I was wrong to chastise you for calling them, and I'm sorry I did that. You were correct to take charge of the situation. On the other hand, I find you are too impulsive. With the job, and with your personal life, the latter of which I do not wish to discuss," Simone said cutting off any discussion about Anthony. "Can't you understand that I had just returned from a long flight, spent the morning in the police station filing charges against Jack, and then received devastating news about Mr. Smith? Instead of giving me some space, you jumped in and took over without any input from me."

Jennifer took a seat in Simone's office, as her partner continued talking. "I could have told you details about the two Chamber parties, instead of calling them, asking why they had called. It seemed very unprofessional. I would have liked to have had the opportunity to call them myself, tell them I had a family emergency, and that my partner would be calling them. That's all I asked."

"But . . ." Jennifer said, only for Simone to raise her hand stopping her from continuing.

"It seemed to me, you were angry because I didn't want to get into a long discussion about Anthony, so you had to get even, and do something you knew would make me angry."

"That's not true," Jennifer interjected.

"Remember when you received the call that our Los Angeles wedding was cancelled?" Simone reminded her. "You didn't tell me until hours later. I believed you were angry because I had suggested you not go out for dinner with Officer Bob Hathaway."

"Sure, I was upset that you didn't want to hear about Anthony because you have this thing about keeping our private lives separate from business life," Jennifer stammered. "I thought you would have been happy for me."

"Happy for you?" Simone responded, trying to keep her tone level. "You tell me you met a guy on a flight, and two weeks later you're moving in with him. You don't see that as impulsive?"

"Well, maybe," she answered, her face flushing slightly.

"Have you made a decision, Jennifer? Are you staying, or moving on?"

"I'm staying. If that's okay with you. I'll try to pay more attention to my actions."

"Jennifer, please understand, I don't care what you do with your personal life, as long as it doesn't affect our work. But when you act out like you did, it impacts me and our business. When we go out, socially, feel free to discuss your personal life, if you'd like. Hearing about Anthony the first thing in the morning, after being out of the office for two weeks, was too much to handle. Do you understand?"

"Yes, I do," Jennifer said, her eyes lowered.

Changing subjects, Simone asked, "Where is everyone? Shouldn't the receptionist be here by now? It's nine-thirty."

Jennifer looked sheepish, and responded. "I told everyone to come in at ten because I needed to talk to you. I know . . . I didn't run that idea past you."

"That's fine, Jennifer. It was a good decision."

"I didn't want the others seeing a hair-pulling, roll-on-the-floor, cat fight in the office," Jennifer joked.

Simone laughed, then added, "Okay, Catwoman, fill me in on what's been going on."

Thirty-Nine

Simone began the weekly Thursday morning staff meeting announcing, "I'm hosting a seven o'clock dinner party at my home next Wednesday, the eighteenth. I hope you all can come. Please, feel free to bring your spouses, your significant others, or dates."

"Oh, that sounds lovely, Simone," Katy responded, her eyes widening with excitement. But, with a bit of disappointment in her voice, she added, "My husband and I have to go to his office holiday party earlier that day, but we can stop by for dessert, if that's okay with you."

Katy was perky and willing to jump in whenever the office got chaotic. Her enthusiasm was nothing less than what Simone expected. She hoped Katy and her husband, a licensed electrician, would come. She knew Charlie was putting out bids for electrical contractors to work at the hotel. It might be a good networking opportunity.

"Yes, coming for dessert is fine," Simone said. "I'd love to meet your husband."

Meanwhile, Jennifer observed Simone. *She certainly is excited about meeting Miss goody-two-shoe's husband. She doesn't show that sort of enthusiasm for meeting Anthony.*

"Jonathan, can you come, too?" Simone asked.

He hesitated. Simone didn't know if he was embarrassed because he didn't have a spouse, or a girlfriend. She and Jennifer exchanged glances. Maybe he was gay, as they had suspected, and wasn't willing to 'come out' to his boss. Simone hoped that wasn't the case. Her internal alarm, 'do not pry' kicked in.

"I think I can make it," he said. "I have to check with my sister. She might need me to babysit."

Simone broke the uncomfortable moment by continuing, "Everyone, just let me know, so I can order enough food. Now, let's get updated on our future events and weddings."

The rest of the day was uneventful. Simone was feeling relieved that no one had broken into her house in months. And, she hadn't received any mysterious text messages for several weeks. Although she had the cameras removed from her house, she kept the panic buttons, with the signal going directly to the ADT monitoring system. Occasionally, she monitored the teddy bear nanny-cam on her iPhone, but the only thing she saw was Anna Maria cleaning her house.

Possibly, the person gave up, and moved on to someone else. Or, it was a high school prank, and they earned their needed 'brownie' points with their gang. Or, the intruder had been staying away since Charlie had been spending most nights at her home. Or, it was Biff, after all, and the stalking died along with him.

Simone didn't want to think about that, or if something much worse was going to happen. The thought gave her a chill.

A few days before the party, Simone purchased a fragrant six-foot Douglas Fir Christmas tree. She pulled ornaments from the attic that she hadn't seen in years. Ornaments, she and Joe had purchased and put on their Christmas trees. The memories were palpable. "Here's to you, Joe," she whispered as she hung a mini Eiffel tower ornament they had purchased on their honeymoon.

Her mantle and tables were decorated with pine garlands, a crèche she and Joe purchased in a small village in France, votive candles, and twinkling lights.

Before the guests arrived, she prepared a fire. She cued her CD player with holiday songs, ready to play at the touch of a button. Silver platters filled with food were covered and waiting in the refrigerator. The dining room table looked elegant, displaying her finest china and glasses, holiday greens, and numerous candles. She was pleased with the effect.

Simone finished getting dressed. She wore her favorite double strand of pearls over a button down green blouse that matched her eyes, a black, wrap around, floor-length skirt, and short leather boots. She reapplied her lipstick, and gave herself a once-over.

Her cell phone sounded, distracting her from her thoughts. It was Jennifer:

*I know I said I would come early to help, but I broke a heel.
Need to go back and change shoes. Will change outfit 'cause
shoes don't match. Sorry. Be there soon.*

Simone looked at her watch. It was five forty-five, plenty of time to do a final inspection of the apartment, and of herself. Hopefully, Jennifer won't be too long. Charlie promised to be here by six, before the guests arrived. She felt giddy, excited, and a bit nervous.

She poured sherry into a Waterford tumbler. She started the fire, and hit the remote to activate the holiday music. She sat on her sofa thinking about how different life is in New England versus Kentucky. Her mind drifted to Judy Smith, and then to her father, Henry. This will be the first Christmas without Mr. Smith. She was thrilled Judy and Mrs. Smith agreed to go to Paris for the holidays. She could relate to the pain and loss, except, Judy truly loved her father.

Her thoughts were broken by a knock on the front door.

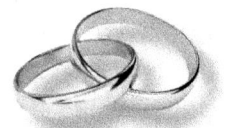

Thirty-Eight

Chief Jacobs informed Simone that Jack confessed to going into her home. He put on her dress, makeup and jewelry, but, he had not stolen Simone's panties, left her flowers, or planted a camera in her lampshade.

The policewoman read his statement over the phone: "I thought about a camera in her bedroom, but I knew she'd call Aldo if she found it," Jack told the police. "I swear, I don't know nothing about stolen underwear."

Simone wasn't happy to hear this news. "I think I'm back at square one, Chief. I surely thought the person who was sending the text messages must be the same person who broke into my home."

"Most likely not, Simone," the Chief said. "Until you figure out another security system, other than your panic buttons, I'd suggest you get an inexpensive camera for your home. Good luck, and remember to call me anytime."

"Thanks," Simone said, hanging up the phone.

She opened her office door, and asked Jonathan to come in. She motioned for him to close the door. "I need your advice on something. I've been having some problems at my home, and I'd like to purchase a nanny-cam. I don't know anything about them . . . where to buy one, cost, etc. Does your sister have one in her house?"

Jonathan was nonplused. He knew Simone's rule on privacy, and didn't intrude by asking any questions. "Yes, she does. They come in all shapes and sizes. And the cost depends on your budget. I can pick one up for you, if you'd like," Jonathan offered.

"Yes, please. That would take a major item off my 'to do' list. And we need to brighten up this office with holiday lights. Do you mind doing these errands?"

"Not at all. Any time I can drive a Porsche, I'm happy."

After discussing her budget, she riffled through her purse. "Here's the company credit card, and the keys to my car." An indescribable jolt went through her body, which she couldn't quite capture. She let it go.

"And yes," she added. "You can buy the holiday lights at Home Depot. But don't get mesmerized by the tools and man-toys," she joked.

Jonathan left her office, promising to return as soon as possible.

Things between her and Jennifer remained strained, but more cordial than a few weeks ago. Jennifer hadn't mentioned Anthony, and Simone hadn't asked about their relationship. No one had broken into her house in weeks, and the text messages seemed to come only in spurts.

Simone felt her text sender was like her father. Calm for a while, and then, 'bam!' a series of text messages, causing heartache and suffering. She reflected on her father, and his abusive outbursts. His anger would build up for a while, and then suddenly, for no reason, he would lash out at her mother, often beating her until she required hospitalization. Then, he would beg for forgiveness, and promise never to hurt her again. Until the next time.

Jennifer knocked at her office door, "Got a second?"

"Sure." Simone welcomed the distraction.

"I'm having a problem with the Christmas Day wedding. The bride can't understand why she's received so many *'Not able to attend'* responses. I'd like to say, 'I told you so' but I'm holding my professional and personal opinion. I'm trying not to be impulsive."

Simone wondered if that was a zing, but she let it go. At least, she thought, Jennifer was trying.

"The couple has been living together for nine years. Plenty of time to plan a beautiful June wedding, but no, she wants to get married on Christmas Day. Even her mother tried talking her out of it. I forewarned her that not everyone wants to go to a wedding on a major holiday, especially this year, when Hanukkah and Christmas are so close together, and Christmas Day is on a Saturday. People would rather be sitting under their decorated tree, opening presents, visiting family and friends, and stuffing their faces with turkey."

Jennifer added, "Her guest list is down to fifty people, and she had to guarantee one hundred twenty-five. She received several offensive notes written on the response cards about the wedding being on Christmas."

Simone answered, "Really? You'd think people would just say, 'no'. Writing such a note on the response card isn't normal. Is the bride difficult or bossy, Jen?"

"Yes. She is to me, to her mother, and to the restaurant manager."

"Where is the venue, again?" Simone asked. "Maybe I can talk to the manager, and see if he can give her a break."

"Thanks. That's what I was hoping. Anything you can do, Simone, would be helpful. Here's the file. Work your magic."

And work it she did. Simone sidestepped the manager, and called the owner of the restaurant directly. She had met him one evening when she was with Charlie. She refreshed his memory on their social interaction.

"Yes, Ms. Simpson, I remember you. How is Charlie?"

"Please, call me Simone. And Charlie's great. Thanks for asking. "Chris, I'm wondering if we could negotiate a workable compromise. Jennifer Keys, my business partner, is working with a bride who is getting married at your restaurant on Christmas Day. Unfortunately, the bride has not reached her minimum number of guests of one hundred twenty-five. She has an attendance list of fifty. Is there something we can agree upon to lower the minimum? I know you haven't ordered the food yet . . ."

"Simone, of course, I can work with you on this. I'm familiar with the situation; my manager has filled me in. I'm sorry the bride isn't able to reach her minimum, but understand, it's not a popular day to hold a wedding. We are usually closed on Christmas, but Steven, the manager, is a good friend of the bride's father. He's willing to open the restaurant in the name of friendship. Trust me, Simone, Steven would prefer to be home with his family that day. He has two small children, and his wife is expecting. The good news is that he can run the wedding with fewer staff than a wedding of one-hundred twenty-five."

"I understand completely, Chris. We had encouraged the bride to consider another date, but she had her heart set on Christmas. And, she wants to hold it at your restaurant. The manager told her father that his hands are tied, and cannot lower the minimum. Our client is in tears. I'm sure you can empathize with her, and understand our position, too. I appreciate your situation and your relationship with Steven. He's just doing his job. This is no fault of his."

Chris stalled for a few minutes, and said, "The best I can do, Simone, is lower the number to one hundred."

"Seventy-five sounds better. It is *Chris*mas, after all."

Chris laughed. "Charlie told me you're a toughie. Now I see what he means. Yes, yes, of course. We would be happy to lower the number to seventy-five."

"And, Charlie told me you're a good man, and a gentleman. Thank you, Chris. My partner, Jennifer Keys will be sending your manager a written confirmation of our agreement. Merry Christmas, and a happy and healthy New Year."

"The same to you, Simone. I look forward to seeing you and Charlie again soon."

Simone walked to Jennifer's desk and handed her the file. "Tell your bride she owes us one. I got her minimum down to seventy-five by promising my first born to the owner of the restaurant," she quipped. "Take full credit for it and keep my name out of it. Send the manager a confirmation letter, so there's no confusion on the minimum. And send Chris Aikens a large holiday fruit basket."

"Simone, thanks for the Christmas Miracle."

"That's why I get paid the big bucks," she retorted. Changing subjects she asked, "Are you going to see your mom and brother on Christmas?"

Jennifer was surprised Simone had asked about her personal life. "Yes. After the wedding, I'll drive out to Long Island for a late dinner with them. My brother will be drunk and sound asleep by that time. What are you and Charlie doing for Christmas?"

Simone hesitated, because she didn't want to reciprocate asking if Anthony was going to Long Island with her. "We're not sure yet." She went back into her office wondering if brides appreciated all that Jennifer and she did to make a wedding day stress free.

Jennifer returned. "You won't believe what that brat said to me. 'You couldn't get it down to less than seventy-five people?' Simone, remind me not to work a Christmas wedding again. I think she is going to be a handful on her wedding day."

"I forgot to ask, is anyone working the wedding with you?"

"No, I'm doing it myself, since it's a manageable guest list, and the ceremony and reception are at the restaurant. In fact, I'm sure that once the reception is underway, and the main course is served, I'll be able to leave."

"Jen, I wanted to ask you something else. I'm thinking of having a small dinner party on the eighteenth. Just for the people in the office, and their significant others. It will be at my house, and I'll have it catered. What do you think?"

"Wow, Simone," Jennifer was astonished. "Nothing but surprises are coming out of you today. Having a dinner party for employees and their significant others . . . very uncharacteristic of you, since you want us to keep our private life secretive. What's gotten into you – the spirit of the holiday season, or too much eggnog?"

Jennifer could always get Simone to react. Since the first day they met at an event planners' conference back in Washington, DC, she was able to get Simone to forget her troubles for just a moment, and bring a smile to her face.

"Well, it actually began a few months ago when Jonathan hung the bulletin board over his desk, and tacked up the photo of his nephew. I realized then, that I didn't know anything about him, or his family life. Nor do I know anything about Katy, other than she's married, has a teenage son who did some website work for us, and lives in Weston. I don't know anything about the receptionist or the temps. I think I should get to know my employees a little bit better. We both should, since you're my partner," Simone said smiling at Jennifer.

She added, "Jonathan said he watches his nephew when his sister has doctor appointments. She was pregnant with her second child, but he never said anything more. I don't know if she had the baby, if she's married, or even if there's a father involved. I wonder if the mother is struggling to make ends meet. Maybe it's the holiday season that's made me sentimental. My husband, Joe, died close to Christmas, so it's always been a tough time of year for me."

"A dinner party would be nice," said Jennifer. "I'll bring appetizers, and come early to help you set up."

"Would you like to bring Anthony?" His name stuck in Simone's throat.

"Thanks for asking. I'll see if he's working that night."

Simone cut her off before Jennifer could regale about Anthony's work. "I'll bring the subject up at our Thursday morning meeting. That gives me three days to change my mind," she joked.

"By the way, have you decided if we are closing the office during Christmas week?" Jennifer asked.

Simone answered, "Jennifer, I've really got the holiday spirit, because I think we should close until the Monday after New Year's. What do you think? We don't have any clients until mid-January, so we could take advantage of the slow season. Charlie and I are flying to Paris on December 23rd and are returning January 8th."

Simone didn't tell Jennifer about the apartment Mr. Smith left her. While in Paris, they'd have the apartment painted, and shop for new furniture. They were excited about spending Christmas in Paris. Judy and Mrs. Smith would be there as well, staying in the apartment next door. Mrs. Smith also hired Irene to stay with them for a full month.

Jennifer stood up, placed her hands on her hips, and in her 6" spike heels towering over Simone, and asked, "Okay, who are you, and what have you done to Simone?"

They laughed.

"Do I have to wear an ugly Christmas sweater to your party?"

"Absolutely," Simone said, giving Jennifer a warm hug.

Forty

"Hi Charlie. It's Jonathan," he said into his cell phone. "Merry Christmas. How are you?"

"I'm great. Merry Christmas to you, too. Are you coming to Simone's dinner party this evening?

"Yes, I am. I might be late, as I have a few gifts to drop off before getting there. I was wondering. . . . I'm in the neighborhood . . . can we share a little holiday cheer, perhaps?"

"That's very nice, Jonathan. I'm here until five-thirty." Charlie hung up the phone, and thought it strange that Jonathan would bring him a holiday gift. He questioned if Jonathan was undermining Simone by approaching her company's vendors. Was he thinking of going out on his own? He was a loyal worker, and, from what he knew about Jonathan, he didn't have the financial backing to start his own business. Charlie dismissed the thought.

Jonathan arrived at four thirty-five, with a box wrapped in holiday paper, which he extended to Charlie. Looking at the size and shape, Charlie assumed it was a bottle of liquor. "This is for you. Merry Christmas," Jonathan said, extending the package to him.

"Thanks Jonathan. That's very thoughtful of you." The men shook hands.

Jonathan's other hand held a cardboard cup holder from Dunkin' Donuts. "I also brought you a cup of coffee. I thought you might need an afternoon pick me up."

Charlie took the second cup and thanked Jonathan for his thoughtfulness. "Cheers," he said, and the men 'clinked' cups. Charlie removed the lid and took a large swallow. They stood bantering for a moment about the traffic this time of year, last-minute shopping . . . mundane subjects. Jonathan asked, "May I sit down?"

"Forgive me, of course. Please," Charlie said, as he motioned to one of his office chairs. He was still confused as to why Jonathan would visit him.

"Is this coffee flavored? It has a distinct aftertaste."

"I think it's their Christmas blend. Drink up – it gets better the more you drink it." Jonathan removed the lid from his cup, and took a large swallow, encouraging Charlie to do the same.

A moment later, Charlie mumbled that he wasn't feeling well, and felt for the chair behind him.

"Give it a moment, Charlie. After a while, you won't feel a thing."

"What are you . . ." Charlie tried to speak, but his tongue felt thick and rigid. His thoughts were jumbled and his eyes couldn't focus. He tried picking up his desk phone, but Jonathan slid it out of his reach.

"Whaaa . . . whaaat . . ." were the only sounds Charlie could utter.

Jonathan sat comfortably in his chair as he watched the powerful drug take hold. Charlie's body moved forward; his head banged against the desk, and soon he was out cold. Jonathan removed several items from his leather messenger bag, and went to work. First, he cut off a large strip of duct tape, lifted Charlie's head off the desk, and fastened the tape across his mouth. "These lips will never again kiss my precious Simone." He placed Charlie's head back on his desk. He used jumbo plastic cable ties to fasten his hands behind his back. "And these hands will never touch her body." Finally, he tied his feet together. "You'll never stand next to her again."

Jonathan removed the gift box and placed it inside his messenger bag. He took a large handful of paper napkins and put them inside Charlie's coffee cup to absorb the remaining liquid. He covered the cup, put it inside his messenger bag, fastened the bag, and strapped it across his chest. He picked up his coffee cup, opened the door, and shut off the office lights. Before leaving, he pushed in the lock button on the doorknob, locking the door behind him. He did a quick perusal of the hallway before he taped a note to Charlie's office door:

Left for the Holiday. See you next year. Happy Holidays. Charlie

He stealthily walked through the lobby and out the front door.

Jonathan headed north on I-95 in bumper-to-bumper holiday traffic. He glanced at the faces of the drivers around him. They looked stressed, agitated, and impatient being stuck in heavy traffic. They were traveling home, or off to visit family for the holiday.

"Fools," he said out loud. "They will never know the magic of Christmas, as I will tonight."

He looked at his watch. It was two minutes after five. At this speed, there was still plenty of time to reach his next destination. He smiled, delighted at how easy it was to take down the one person who stood in his way of success.

Forty-One

Simone opened the front door, expecting to see Charlie.

Instead, she faced an oversized bouquet of red roses, making her heart skip a beat. "Jonathan," she said as she looked past the flowers.

The cold air turned his breath to fog, as if he were smoking a cigarette. His eyes twinkled. "Merry Christmas. I hope you don't mind that I came early."

"That's fine. Come on in." She got a slight whiff of his cologne as he walked past her.

She closed the door behind him, leaving it unlocked.

She was rattled by the bouquet. She remembered the long stem roses left in her kitchen by the intruder. But she quickly recovered.

"Thank you for the flowers," she said, although the words stuck in her throat.

"Well, I'm not much of a cook, and I know every woman loves flowers."

"They're lovely." She placed them on the kitchen counter.

"You have a beautiful home, Simone."

"Thank you."

She noticed he also had a small box under his arm, wrapped in festive Christmas paper. He removed his coat, but left his cashmere scarf on around his neck. The plaid Burberry pattern, along with his black turtleneck, complimented his skin tone.

"Where can I can hang my coat, and may I use your restroom?"

"My closets are full, so, just put it on the bed in the master bedroom, and you can use the en suite."

Before she could utter the words, "Down the hall on your left," he headed towards her room, as if he knew his way.

"The light switch is on the wall out. . ." but this too, she didn't finish saying. His fingers flipped the switch, turning on the light inside her bedroom. She stood and stared at his back. How did he know the switch was *outside* the bedroom, and not *inside?* Changing the location of the switch was something she regretted not having done when she had the house renovated. Jonathan stopped. He turned, and smiled. The twinkle was gone.

A flash of fear ran through her. She had three bedrooms, yet he knew exactly which was the master. Her mind raced. Her heart thumped. Her mouth became parched. Her hands began shaking.

As if finding the solution to a mind-bending puzzle, the pieces suddenly, and systemically came together. She deciphered the algorithm, the procedure, the chain of events. It was logical. It all made sense now. Her mind raced over the past several months, and the invasions.

How could he have gotten a key to my house? I never gave him one. And then she remembered the uneasy feeling she felt when she handed him her car keys to buy holiday lights.

The details suddenly became clear. *Jonathan had driven my car to pick up the invitations for the White wedding before the printer closed for the weekend. I was stuck in the office with clients. He must have made a copy of my house key, which was on the keyring along with my car key. Shortly after, my underwear was stolen. He knew I was with Jennifer in Seattle.*

She continued to muse. *After I changed the lock, he took my car to the Porsche dealer. Or, did he? Maybe he was releasing air out of my tire, hoping he would get his hands on my keys again. He took the car to the gas station to get air. He knew how busy I was with the Bradshaw wedding, and that I wouldn't have had the time to take care of the problem. There wasn't a nail in the tire. That's why Sal had no record in the computer system. From there, he went to Home Depot to purchase the bulletin board, but he also made a copy of the replacement key, installed by Jack. That's when he left the roses. Again, he knew I was at Jennifer's father's funeral. And, I was stupid enough to ask him to go to Home Depot to purchase a new tumbler for my lock. He must have had an extra key made once again. Adding to that, I asked for his recommendation on a nanny-cam, and asked him to take my car — again — and purchase it for me. By now, he's discovered the cam in my bedroom.*

Simone felt a sliver of dread pierce through her. *Jonathan was the one who had come into my house, and had planted the camera in my lampshade. He thought I was at lunch with Marissa from the Chamber, and then, at IKEA. He didn't know I had a loaner car. Or, that I was hiding under my bed.*

Did he kill Biff? Barbara said the call came from inside the hotel. Jonathan said he wanted to get a date with the receptionist. Was it a ploy, simply to get away from Jennifer and me? Had he ordered the cookies, using the lobby phone so it couldn't be traced back to his room?

She needed to keep busy while she ran a litany of questions through her mind. *What if I am wrong, and falsely accuse him? It would be a huge embarrassment, and he would probably quit, and try to ruin my reputation.*

Simone took down her crystal vase, the same one that held the intruder's flowers. She removed the roses from their paper holder. She opened the utility drawer, and saw two items that would save her from her escalating fear. Simone relied on her intuition and took advantage of both.

She removed her floral sheers, began cutting the stems of the flowers, and placing them inside the crystal vase, running the events through her mind, once again. And again. She was convinced that it was just her imagination. But her mind continued to come up with solutions to every question.

Jonathan knew Biff was allergic to hazelnuts. Every meal delivered from room service came with complimentary cookies, some with Nutella in them. He could have requested cookies with the chocolate spread, along with the champagne, to be delivered to the groom's room, hoping Biff would eat a cookie. It was a risk, but it worked.

Barbara mentioned she was missing a pair of panties, Biff's favorite. When the three of us went to their apartment, Jonathan used the bathroom in the master bedroom. I wonder if he took a pair of her panties, too, not knowing they would be missed because they were her favorite. Could it all be a coincidence? I don't believe in coincidences. She shuddered as these thoughts kept coming.

*Was it Jonathan, and not Biff, sending me text messages? I trust
. . . no, trusted Jonathan; he's a loyal employee.* He came to the business, along with Katy. *I never did a background check on them as
I did on the other employees, including Jennifer. How foolish. How
irresponsible. How stupid.*

Simone's stomach turned. It seemed Jonathan was in her bedroom
for a long time. *Was he in the bathroom, or doing something else? Should
I go to the bedroom and check?* she thought. An important fact she learned
in self-defense flashed through her mind: *never go to a second location.*
In the kitchen she was closest to the front door. The master bedroom
was further away from an escape route.

Simone ran the events through her mind again. And again. She
tried convincing herself that she was wrong. *Jonathan is like a brother
to me. He would never do anything to harm me. He saved me from
Biff's attack.*

No matter how many times she reconstructed the events, she came
up with the same answer. *Yes, Jonathan had to be the one.* She no longer
doubted herself.

Simone quickly thought of texting Jennifer, telling her to call the
police and that she was in trouble. But her cell phone was in the master
bedroom. *What if Jonathan saw my phone on the nightstand, and hid
it from me? Maybe I should leave and run to Cynthia's house? But that
would give him time to leave, and deny my accusations. Or worse, what if
he set my house on fire.*

Her hands began trembling. She decided the best recourse was to
get out of her house. She'd run to Cynthia's, and get help.

She smelled him before she felt him.

Forty-Two

"You look lovely, Simone," Jonathan whispered in her ear.

She jumped, dropping the sheers on the counter. His breath emitted a warm flow of air against her ear and neck. Conversely, a cold chill ran through her body.

She turned to face him. He was inches from her face. "Thank you," she said, her voice quivering.

She needed to buy time. Her mind raced as to how to get out of this situation. All doubts and questions about Jonathan being her stalker melted away. There were no more doubts - she was convinced. Now, she needed to put those questions out of her mind and focus on how she was going to handle this situation. She had to stall, until Charlie arrived. Questions of: *what if he was running late, or was stuck in traffic, or a client came to visit,* raced through her mind. She chided herself. *Focus on the present moment.*

Jonathan placed his hands on both sides of Simone's body, pinning her to her kitchen counter. At the same time, he placed his feet between her legs, and pushed them out, as far as her legs would go. Jonathan pushed his body up against hers, causing her head to bang against the upper cabinet. She couldn't move left or right. She was pinned.

Her self-defense training crossed her mind, but Jonathan was very familiar with those techniques, as he had taken the same classes. She knew she was in deep trouble.

The lower part of her body was useless, as if tied in a straitjacket. She raised her hands, but he quickly grabbed them.

"No, Simone. Not this time. You're not going to get yourself out of this situation. You were able to take down Biff, but he wasn't as strong as I am. He needed to be removed."

"Did you kill him, Jonathan?" Simone asked, trying to stall. *Conversation. Start a conversation with him.* "Why did you kill him? How did you kill him?"

"Of course I killed him. He touched you. Anyone who has touched you must die."

A rush of fear shot through her body, unlike any she had ever known before. Her heart pounded in her chest.

"Charlie. What have you done to Charlie?"

The twinkle was back, along with a sinister smile. "Don't worry about Charlie. He won't bother you ever again, Simone. Now, you belong to me." He held her wrists together with one hand, while he removed his scarf. As he tied her hands together behind her back, he pushed his body against her even harder.

"Jonathan, please don't do this. No one is here yet, just leave. I won't say anything to anyone. I promise. I'll make an excuse for you . . . you called and said you had to babysit after all. Please. Just don't do this."

"It is time, Simone."

"Time?"

"Yes. Be quiet," he said. "I don't want to have to tape your mouth shut. Besides, no one will hear your screams over the music. No, that mouth . . . the mouth I've longed to kiss for years."

He removed her pearl necklace, and placed it on the counter. He began to unbutton her blouse, while he kissed her mouth, then her neck. He removed her blouse, and pulled it down around her hands.

Simone began to cry, begging him to stop.

He unhooked her bra. He moaned a throaty sound of delight, "You're so beautiful, Simone." He cupped his hands around her breasts, caressing them. "No one will ever touch your breasts again. You are mine. From the first day I saw you, I've wanted you. You have no idea what torture it's been watching you from my desk, to see you every day, to see you with that monster. That monster who touched you, who kissed you, who made love to you. No one will ever do that to you again. Except me."

"Help!" Simone screamed.

Jonathan brutally slapped her across the face. Fury masked his face, his eyes wild. "Don't make me tape your mouth shut, Simone."

Her face stung from the slap. Her jaw began to throb. Fear, disgust and memories of horror filled her mind. Memories of her father's abuse surfaced.

Simone cried, "Please, Jonathan, stop. Please, before this goes too far."

"I've dreamed of this day for years. I'm not stopping now. I love you, Simone. You are more beautiful than I ever imagined. He began thrusting his pelvis in a grinding motion. She could feel his erection. Her father's face flashed in front of her eyes.

"Stop, Jonathan. Stop." Tears ran down her face that made her mascara create black lines down to her chin.

"You are mine." His breathing increased. "Say you will be mine forever."

Simone's mind raced in absolute horror. He was going to rape her, and then, most likely, kill her. She had to do something. Her hands frantically moved as one force, unable to do anything.

He held her face tightly in his hands, bringing renewed pain where he slapped her. He kissed her with passion, forcing his tongue into her mouth. "I love you. Now, you will be mine, the way it was meant to be."

He unwrapped her skirt, and threw it aside. He pushed down her panties.

Simone cried louder, begging him to stop. The same old fears and horror washed over her. She was reliving the nightmare of her father raping her when she was twelve years old. The scene ran in her mind, over and over again.

She moved her hands back and forth, trying to loosen the scarf, but it was tied too tightly. Her hands groped behind her for anything she could use as a weapon. They stopped when she felt the sheers . . . cold and sharp.

"And now, you will be mine." His brown eyes were wild, the flickering holiday lights reflecting off them.

"Please, Jonathan." She tried another tact. "Please, untie my hands. I can't feel them, they're going numb. I'm in pain. Please, Jonathan. You don't want to hurt me, do you?"

"No, Simone. I don't want to hurt you. I'm sorry I had to slap you, but if you make noise I will be forced to hurt you again. I love you. I want to make love to you. I've already prepared our bed for our night of lovemaking."

"Then please, untie my hands." She continued her path of thinking. He was either going to kill her, or believe her. "You know it's not fair, what you're doing."

"What's not fair?" he said as he continued to kiss her breasts. His hands and fingers began exploring between her thighs.

"I can't feel you," she said, in a sensual tone. "I didn't think you felt the connection between us, Jonathan. I dropped hints, but you never picked up on them."

He stopped kissing her, and looked at her. "Hints? What hints?"

She spoke softly, with conviction. "For starters, I gave you a bonus. I never give any of my employees a bonus. Didn't that tell you that I liked you? I invited you to go to Paris with me. I took you to my very special places in Paris, places I only went to with my husband. Remember the candlelight dinners? The boat ride down the Seine? All the romantic places. You even said you felt the romance in the air."

Her mind raced. "Then there's Biff. I knew what time you would be leaving your room, to meet us downstairs. I invited Biff to my room, and tried to seduce him." She hoped he was believing her. "I wanted to make you jealous. I left my hotel door open, hoping you would hear me. I pretended he had attacked me, but in reality, he refused to make love to me. Remember I said you showed up at the exact moment?"

"I don't believe you. What about Jennifer. She was with us."

"I hate that bitch!" Simone spit the words with as much conviction she could muster.

"What? That's not true. You're lying. You and Jennifer are close."

"Don't you remember how disappointed she was when I said the wedding didn't warrant having three of us?" Jonathan nodded, trying to see if what Simone was saying made sense or was logical.

His fingers began exploring her again.

Simone closed her eyes, trying to force away the horror. She opened them again, her green eyes locked on his.

"She and I got into a huge fight over you. She didn't want to stay behind. She likes you, Jonathan. She calls you eye candy because she thinks you're hot. She wants you, too. She didn't want us to be alone in Paris. I would have had you all to myself. Just you and me," she whispered. She could tell his excitement was increasing. "Why do you think she shared my room? She didn't trust me. She thought I would invite you into my bed."

Jonathan's eyes narrowed. "I still don't believe you. You're making this up. Why didn't you say something sooner? Why are you telling me now?"

"Because I didn't think you wanted me. You've always kept your distance. Remember you tried to comfort me after Biff attacked me? I was hoping you would have held me in your arms, so I could feel your body against mine. But you gently put your arm around my shoulder, and quickly took it away. I believed you didn't want me. But now, you're proving to me that you do. I want you too, Jonathan."

"You're lying."

Simone pressed on. "Have I ever lied to you, Jonathan? Jennifer wants you, just like I want you. Think about it. The three of us together at once. Tonight. Soon."

He hesitated. Maybe she was getting through to him.

His fingers stopped for a moment. He was thinking. A flash of excitement lit up his eyes with added sexual excitement, at the thought of having two women.

"Yes. All of it. I've never lied to you Jonathan. Never. I wanted you all to myself in Paris, but she came between us. She paid her own way, just to keep us apart."

Simone studied his face, to see if he was buying her story. "Jonathan, please, I'm begging you. Untie my hands. I want to feel you, too."

"What about Charlie? You claim to be in love with him."

"Jonathan, I'm using Charlie. Using him to get good rates for our brides, for your events, for us. He doesn't live with me. He spends his money on me, buying me gifts, taking me out to fancy restaurants. He means nothing to me. Don't you think we'd be married by now, or living together? I keep putting him off. It is you I want. Please, Jonathan. Please untie my hands."

He reached behind Simone, and freed her hands. "No funny business."

"No, I swear." Once her hands were untied she let her blouse and bra fall to the ground. "Thank you so much."

Her self-defense training had taught her that in rare situations, it was best to be nice to the attacker. Make them feel as if you cared about them.

She responded by sliding her hands up his chest, and wrapped her arms around his neck. She leaned in and kissed him with convincing passion. "That's so much better, isn't it?"

"Yes," he said, kissing her again with equal vigor and determination.

"Let me see your body. I want to touch you, too."

He hesitated, but he removed his turtleneck.

She continued her playacting. "Oh, Jonathan, you're gorgeous. More. I want to see all of you. Then we can make love."

He released her legs and unzipped his pants, and let them fall around his ankles. He was not wearing underpants. He kicked off his shoes, and bent down to remove his pants, tossing them to the side.

As he bent down, Simone's hand felt for the sheers.

Simone met his eyes, and whispered, "Let me see you. I want to see your whole body."

Jonathan was very proud of his body, and all his hard work at the gym to achieve an attractive physic. He took two steps back, and she drank in his naked body.

"Oh Jonathan, I've dreamed of this day for so long. You are breathtaking." As she said the words, her right hand wrapped around the floral sheers.

"I keep in shape just for you, Simone. Only for you."

"Your body is magnificent." She needed to break eye contact. She had to get him to look away. She looked down at his enlarged manhood.

"You promised you would not hurt me, but looking at you . . . you're so large . . . I'm so afraid." She smiled at him.

He looked down at his manhood, with complete satisfaction, elated that Simone liked what she saw. He cupped his genitals in his hands, as if showing it off like a trophy. He smiled.

At that moment, Simone's right hand swung around, and using all the rage, horror and strength left in her body, slammed the sheers into his chest.

His eyes went wide with shock and fear. He stared at her, as pain rushed up his spinal cord and hit his brain. Then, she launched the final blow – a boot kick to his quickly deflating penis. Jonathan's arms spiraled as his body fell backward. He hit the ceramic tile floor with a loud thud. Blood poured out of his head and chest.

He was dead.

She heard scurrying footsteps arriving at her house. Then a blast of cold air slammed against her naked body. The police charged in, and drew their guns. Simone extended her hands as she slumped down onto the floor, her body drained of any adrenaline, energy, or ability to fight any longer.

She awoke minutes later, her body covered with a throw blanket from the sofa. Chief Jacobs had her arms around her, waving smelling salts under her nose.

"Simone. Simone. Are you okay?"

"What happened?" Her eyes fluttered in an effort to stay open. "Jonathan . . . oh my God . . . Jonathan . . . he was going to kill me."

"You are one lucky woman. Let's get you to the sofa."

Chief Jacobs and another female officer helped Simone up, walking her over to the couch. Simone could hear additional sirens, running footsteps, and the cacophony of radio static.

As she walked past the gruesome scene in her kitchen, she looked at Jonathan's naked, dead body.

She whispered, "Yes, people do die around me."

Forty-Three

Jennifer arrived shortly after the police, her arms full of platters of appetizers.

"I'm sorry, Miss. You can't go in there. You'll have to leave."

"I'm Jennifer Keys, Simone's business partner and friend."

Simone quietly whispered, "Jennifer?"

The Police Chief nodded to the officer standing guard at the door, giving permission for Jennifer to enter. Jennifer left the platters of food on a side table near the door, and ran to Simone. She glanced over at Jonathan's naked body. His eyes were open and expressionless. The twinkle was gone, forever. His head rested in a pool of dark blood, releasing a metallic smell mixed with urine and fecal matter. A pair of floral sheers protruded from his blood-covered chest.

"Simone, are you all right?" Jennifer turned away in revulsion.

An officer called from Simone's bedroom, "Chief, you need to see this," he said as he waved her on to the master bedroom. The Chief instructed Jennifer to continue waving the smelling salts under Simone's nose. "We need her awake to tell us what happened."

"Simone, can you hear me? Simone, where's Charlie? I thought he was going to be here. Simone."

"Charlie?" Suddenly, fear gripped Simone. She struggled to organize her scrambled thoughts. She remembered something that Jonathan said . . . 'he won't bother you again.' With every ounce of energy she looked at Jennifer and whispered, "He said Charlie must die." Simone burst into tears as her friend held her in her arms.

The Police Chief returned. "How's she doing?"

Jennifer gestured toward the dead body. "Jonathan told her that Charlie must die." Without coming up for air, she rapidly said, "He's

Simone's boyfriend. Can you look for him? His full name is Charles Hamilton. He's the general manager at the Grand Hamilton Hotel in Greenwich. He also lives there."

"Yes, I've met him before," Jacobs said.

"Call Officer McGuire, Greenwich Police," Simone managed to whisper.

A rookie cop, standing nearby, heard the conversation. The Chief nodded to him, and the officer got on his cell phone. Simone heard him say, ". . . possible homicide," and she burst into fresh tears.

The Chief gave the rookie cop a warning look, as to say, 'not here'.

"Simone, are you able to stand up?"

"Where's Charlie?" she begged Jennifer and the Chief.

"We have officers looking for Charlie now."

The Chief turned to Jennifer, "Can we talk?"

Jennifer put an arm around Simone's shoulder and assured her that she would be close by. "The policewoman needs to talk to me," she explained.

Jennifer grabbed tissues from her purse and handed them to her friend. Simone nodded as fresh waves of sobs came forth.

The officer instructed Jennifer, "I need you to go into Simone's bedroom and get an outfit from her closet. Do not, under any circumstances, open any dresser drawers. Understand?" She lowered her voice even more. "We don't know if he's rigged the drawers in any way, and we won't know until we get a dog in here."

Jennifer was stunned, hearing the chilling words.

"Do not touch anything other than pants, and a top. There is an officer in there now, taking photographs. Tell him what you need. I repeat, do not open any dresser drawers. Her dark brown eyes were serious and piercing. "I also have to warn you that the scene is upsetting. So please keep your reaction as passive as possible. Can you do that?"

"Yes, I think so." Jennifer said. "I know Simone has a box of clothes in her closet that she wears when she travels. Can I look for the box? It will have underwear in it."

"Yes. Ask the officer in there for help."

Jennifer entered Simone's bedroom, and faced a terrifying sight. Her bedsheets were turned down, as if ready to accept an evening of lovemaking. There were rose petals on the floor, and on her bed. Intermingled on her pillows and sheets were dozens of pairs of panties. She wondered if a pair of Barbara Kemp's underwear was in the mix.

Tossed in the corner of the floor was an empty gift box. Along the side of the bed were two pairs of handcuffs, duct tape, a large knife, and a rope. At the foot of the bed was Simone's nanny-cam. The teddy bear's head was partially chopped off, like a bobble head with a broken spring. She walked into the closet, and with the help of the police officer got the clothes she needed, and quickly brought them to Simone.

By then, Simone was able to stand and regain her composure. Jennifer walked her friend to the hall bathroom. Along the way, she blocked Simone's view from the terrifying site only yards away in her bedroom.

Simone looked in the mirror at an ashen face covered with black mascara streaks. Her skin was blotchy and her eyes hollow. She washed her face, the sting of Jonathan's slap reminding her of the night's horrors.

Jennifer continued. "The Chief wants to talk to you when you're up to it. And they want to take you to hospital for observation."

"I don't need to go to the hospital. I need Charlie." Simone burst into tears again. "Jennifer, if Jonathan killed him, I'll never forgive myself."

"Shh, don't say that," her friend said, putting her arms around Simone. I'm sure Charlie is fine. I think the police are concerned you hit your head, and your jaw is swollen. They want to observe you overnight. Does your head hurt?"

"No. When I started to feel faint I sat down, so I don't think I hit my head. I banged it against the cabinets when Jonathan had me pinned . . . oh Jennifer, if was absolutely horrible. He was going to kill me. He was the one who stole my underwear, who broke into my house, and I believe, the one who sent the text messages."

"How, Simone? How could he get in here so many times?" Jennifer inquired.

"Remember he picked up the White invitations, he took my car to the dealer, and he bought the lock for me, and the holiday lights?" Jennifer nodded. "He drove my car. My house key was on the same keyring. He made copies each time." Simone began to cry again. "And, he killed Biff."

"What? How? Never mind. I'll hear about that later, when you tell the police the full story about what happened tonight. Are you able to talk to the police? I'll be by your side. I'm here for you."

"Yes, I'm ready," she said stoically.

Throngs of neighbors were huddled by the front gate. The police had a difficult time keeping inquiring minds from asking questions, or peering inside her home. The local news truck, with a large satellite dish on its roof, parked across the street. Whispers and unfounded rumors were circulated. The police dispersed the crowd, and secured the area around her house with yellow caution tape.

A K-9 unit arrived, and a large German Shephard padded its way into Simone's house. "It's procedure," said the officer.

Jennifer wondered if the police saw something suspicious in Simone's bedroom to cause them to bring in a dog.

"How did you know to come," Jennifer asked the Chief?

"Yes, how *did* you know?" asked Simone.

"The panic button saved your life. Don't you remember pressing it?"

Simone hesitated for a moment, trying to recall the events. "Yes, I do remember, now."

Simone proceeded to tell Jacobs and Jennifer the whole story . . . how Jonathan showed up early with a big bouquet of roses. She explained how he knew the location of her bedroom, and where the light switch was - outside the room, not inside. Only someone who's been in her bedroom would know.

That's when she started to recall it all. While he was in her bedroom, she opened the utility drawer to get the floral sheers, to arrange the flowers. She saw the panic button. "I remembered what you told me: We'd rather it be a false alarm than a tragedy."

"Well, I'm glad someone listens to me," the Chief said, trying to lighten the mood. "When we received the call that the panic button was activated, and your home address came across the screen, I thought you had another intruder."

"I still want you to go to the hospital for evaluation," said the officer. "You have red marks on your face and wrists. EMS is here and they can do a preliminary check." Lowering her voice to a whisper, out of earshot of the other officers, she asked, "Did he rape you, Simone?"

"No, Chief. He didn't. But I do believe that would have been his next move, before killing me."

"I still want you to go to hospital to be checked. You don't have to go, but, if EMS recommends a hospital visit, please Simone, go."

At 7:30, the Coroner's van pulled up. They tagged and bagged Jonathan's body, and removed him.

In Paris, Jonathan said he never wanted his body to be taken out in a body bag. He should have thought of that before going up against Simone.

Forty-Four

"Please let me in. I'm a close friend. Please." The commotion outside Simone's house grew louder, with police officers threatening to arrest the man who insisted on seeing Simone.

"Chief, there's a guy . . ."

"Simone, I'm here to help. Simone, let me in. Please."

"Pete. That's Pete's voice," Simone said. "Oh please, let him in. He's a good friend." The officers let him pass, and Simone fell into his arms. "Oh Pete. Thank goodness you're here."

Jennifer looked at the Police Chief, and shrugged her shoulders. The Chief whispered, "Then, how does Charlie fit into her life?" Jennifer had never met or heard of Pete before. She certainly wasn't aware of their relationship, which seemed overly friendly.

"Simone, are you injured?" he questioned.

"Pete, I'm fine, now that you and Jennifer are here," she said warmly. Jennifer sized him up to be in his late thirties, balding, and he wasn't wearing a wedding band. She stepped forward.

"Hi, I'm Jennifer Keys, Simone's business partner," Jennifer said extending her hand. "Thank you for coming to check on Simone. How do you know her?"

"I've known Simone since she purchased this house. I did the construction on the renovations. Don't you remember me?"

Jennifer took a closer look at the man standing in front of her. Several years had passed. He was a few pounds heavier, and a few hairs lighter. She had casually met him when Simone was having the work done, but never paid much attention to him.

"Pete, I'm going to need your help," Simone said. She ran her fingers through her curls, brushed her hands down her pants, and within seconds, Simone morphed into her event planner mode, handling an emergency with her usual intellect and determination. She always knew what to do, and this was the worst emergency she had ever faced. Jennifer had seen Simone's transformation in the past, but this was palpable. Even the police were awed.

"As you can see, there's blood all over my kitchen. I need the kitchen redone, new cabinets, new ceramic tile floor, and new appliances. Gut it. I'll e-mail you photos of what I'd like. And, can you redo my bedroom? New bedroom set, rug, new everything. In fact, I don't use the other bedrooms. Take one, and incorporate it into a large master suite with a sitting room. We can design a way to close off the sitting area if I ever need a third bedroom."

"Absolutely. No problem. Anything you want," Pete said, occasionally glancing over at the Police Chief.

Simone headed towards her master bedroom with Pete in tow, but the Police Chief stopped her. "Let Pete see your plans another day, Simone. Officers are busy in there." Chief Jacobs said. She gave Pete a stern look. Unspoken words were understood, and Pete got the message.

"I can stop by after the holidays and we can design your new kitchen and master bedroom then," Pete said.

"Great. I knew I could count on your help. You'll have to coordinate with Police Chief Jacobs, as to when you can get in here. I'll be staying at the Grand Hamilton Hotel in Greenwich until the 23rd, then Charlie and I are leaving for Paris. I won't be back until after the New Year. You can get a lot of the work done during that time."

Simone's holiday travel plans were news to Jennifer. She had to admit, it was impressive watching her boss taking charge and giving orders.

She continued, "And Pete, when everything is complete, I'll need a new lock on my front door."

Jennifer thought Simone was in shock. Saying she was staying at the Hamilton Hotel without knowing about Charlie's status, convinced Jennifer that Simone didn't realize the full impact of what just happened to her. Why wasn't she focused on Charlie? What was happening? And who is this Pete? She wasn't convinced he was the same person she had met years ago.

"Where's Charlie?" Pete asked.

"The police are looking for him." Simone's eyes filled. "Oh Pete, if anything happened to him, I'll never forgive myself." She wrapped her arms around his waist, feeling comfortable and safe. Pete rested his cheek on Simone's head, a position that was familiar to both of them, and obvious to those watching.

Pete whispered words of support. Seeing the two of them embraced made Jennifer suspect that Pete was more than just a contractor. There must have been a relationship between them in the past. Or, even now.

Simone pulled away, and looked into his eyes. "Pete, please don't tell the neighbors what has happened tonight. And, I never want to ask anyone to keep a secret from their spouse, but in this case, I need you to keep this from your wife."

Ah, so he is married, Jennifer realized.

"I won't. I must admit, Joyce is a blabbermouth. She's my wife, and I love her, but she gossips. No problem, Simone." Pete turned to the Chief, extending a handshake. "Thank you for allowing me to talk to Simone. I've worked crime scenes before. I know what needs to be done. I'll get in touch with you next week." He turned to Simone, gave her a hug and a light kiss on the cheek. "I hope Charlie is fine. Keep me posted."

Simone remembered the food sitting in her refrigerator. She noticed Jennifer's platters of appetizers near the front door. The table was set, and ready for a feast. "Pete," she called after him. "Take platters of food home to Joyce and the kids. And Chief, please tell your officers to take the food out of the refrigerator, and help themselves, too."

"Thank you Simone," Pete said. He grabbed a couple of trays of food before leaving.

The rookie cop bolted into in the living room announcing, "They found him, Chief," the officer said. "Charles Hamilton. They found him."

"Is he dead?" asked Simone, on the verge of fainting again.

Indeed, she was in shock.

Forty-Five

"This is Sargent Franco with the Westport Police Department. May I speak with Detective McGuire?"

"I'm sorry, but Detective McGuire has left for the holidays. May I help you?" asked the desk sergeant.

"We've had a home invasion in Westport, and the homeowner, Ms. Simone Simpson, has specifically requested McGuire to help with this case. We are searching for Charles Hamilton at the Grand Hamilton Hotel. Are you familiar with the facility?"

"Yes, I am. In fact, I believe McGuire and Powers were involved in a homicide at the hotel about a year ago."

Franco explained the situation at Simone's home, and the urgency of finding Charles Hamilton.

"I'll text McGuire with details, and see if he is still in town. Are we talking about Hamilton Senior, or Junior?"

"The general manager who goes by Charlie. I believe he lives at the hotel – has a room there."

"Okay, that's Charlie, the son," the desk sergeant said. "We'll get right on it, Franco. Someone will get back to you shortly."

Powers, still on duty, along with another officer, headed to the hotel.

"How may I help you?" asked the tall blond male staff member. "I'm Frederick Murphy."

"Aren't you the one that was shot the day we took Hathaway into custody?" asked Officer Powers

Frederick, Charlie's nephew was hit by a bullet as he tried to flee a crowded conference room during the Robert Hathaway interrogation, a security guard at the hotel. Frederick, Hathaway, the bride and the groom, knew each other years before when they had all attended Princeton.

Frederick's family owned the hotel. His mother was Charlie's sister. After he was fired by his uncle, Charlie's father rehired Frederick, but put him in charge of the staff at the registration desk and housekeeping. Until Frederick could prove himself again, Charlie didn't want any interaction with him. Tonight, because a large number of staff were gone for the holiday, Frederick had to work until midnight. So when he saw the two police officers enter the lobby, he assumed that this would turn out to be an exciting night, after all.

"We're looking for Charles Hamilton," said Officer Powers.

"What is this . . ." but Frederick stopped mid-sentence. He knew his uncle would be furious if he took command of a situation. "I'll see if he's in his office."

Forty-Six

Charlie woke to the earsplitting sound of a phone ringing. He tried moving his head, but it felt as if it weighed a hundred pounds. He had the worst headache of his life. Was he having a stroke? Why couldn't he answer the phone?

Finally, the ringing stopped.

Charlie went back to sleep.

"I'm sorry, there's no answer in his office. I'll try his suite." After a few seconds, Frederick gave the officers the same response.

"Can we see his office?" Powers asked.

That old familiar 'take charge' emotion stirred in Frederick's belly. Finally, after so many months, he was in charge again. He reminded himself to be careful. He stood up straight, his 6'6" height towering over the two officers. "Follow me."

Charlie heard the banging on his office door, the doorknob twisting, words of 'gone for the holiday' and 'he's not here.' He tried to speak, but his tongue was swollen, and there was tape across his mouth. His eyes couldn't focus through the blurry haze. In the darkened room, he couldn't tell if he had lost his eyesight, or if it was the effect of the drug.

Simone. He had to warn Simone. How long had he been here, he wondered? He tried lifting his head, but it swirled. His neck was cramped from his head lying on the desk for so long. Thoughts of Jonathan, the coffee, and Simone, floated in his mind.

He was so tired. *If I got some sleep, maybe I'll have strength.*

He closed his eyes again. He heard his cell phone ringing.

Franco and Powers updated Frederick on the details of what had happened at Simone's home, and how they feared Jonathan may have harmed Charlie. Frederick radioed all hotel personnel to be on the look-out for Charlie. If anyone saw him, they needed to radio Frederick immediately. The trio went up to Charlie's suite and inspected every inch of the apartment. There wasn't a trace that anyone had been in the room for several hours.

On the dresser were two gifts, addressed to Simone and Jennifer. Officer Powers said, "It looks like Charlie hadn't left the hotel to go to Simone's house. Otherwise, he would have taken the gifts with him. So he's got to be here in this hotel. Let's keep looking."

Frederick called the front desk and asked for the two supervisors to meet him and the officers by the elevators. There, Frederick instructed the two to split up, one going through the guests' amenities, checking the pools, the tennis courts, the game room, and the spa. "Get a bell hop, waiters, or maintenance to help you . . . anyone. And update me every five minutes. Ask the front desk to look through the hotel security system to see if Charlie shows up on the tape." Frederick was back in charge, and it felt good.

They left the elevators and were heading to the grand ballroom, when Frederick stopped short. The two officers looked at him. Frederick frowned.

"What is it? Do you know something?" asked Sargent Franco.

"There was something about the note Charlie taped to the door. I can't put my finger on it. Let's head to the kitchens."

The chef was startled when he saw Frederick and two police officers invade his immaculate cooking space, opening cabinets and doors, turning over pots and pans. "What is going on?" demanded the head chef, obviously annoyed at the raid.

"We are looking for Charles Hamilton . . . he's missing. Foul play is suspected," Frederick said.

"We need to check the walk-in refrigerator," commanded Officer Powers. A moment of silence hung heavily over the room. Sous chefs stopped chopping, dish washers turned off the water, waiters froze with dishes balanced on their arms. All eyes were on the chef as he led the three men to the walk-in freezer.

There, hanging from a large industrial hook was a burlap bag, tied at the top, with a large bulge protruding from the bottom.

"Uncle Charlie!" cried Frederick.

"No. No. Freddie, your imagination has taken the best of you," said the chef. "That's this morning's delivery. I would have seen someone carrying in a body. No one goes into my freezer without my permission. Ask anyone." A quick look around at the nodding heads of the workers, told the officers the freezer was a sanctuary entered only by the head chefs.

The chef took a large cleaver and ripped open the bag. Out fell the slaughtered body of a small calf. "Milk-fed veal," the chef said, puffing out his chest as if he was showing off a trophy.

The three men left the kitchen, and walked into the adjacent banquet hall.

"Could Charlie have left the premises?" one of the officers asked.

"Security is reviewing the hotel tapes now. We should know soon." Frederick remembered being in the interrogation room, when he learned about the security cameras. They were installed on his days off because his uncle didn't trust him to keep his mouth shut. At the time, someone working at the hotel was stealing jewelry and prescription medications from the guests, and Charlie was determined to find the culprit without Frederick tipping them off. *I hate to admit it, but my uncle was right. I did let my authority get the best of me. I'd do anything now to find him.*

For the next twenty minutes, every valet, housekeeper, bellhop and waiter looked for Charlie. They explored every closet, conference room, storage room, broom closet, banquet hall, and empty guest room. Security personnel knocked on the doors, and inspected each room. Staff, who owned 4x4 cars searched the three hundred acre estate, looking under every bush, up in trees, and navigated their way around the mounds of snow looking for footprints. The results were the same in every nook and cranny of the large estate. Charlie was nowhere to be found.

The static emanating from Frederick's radio startled the three men. "Frederick, this is Manny at the front desk. Security found footage of a man going into Charlie's office. I recognized him as the events planner a few months ago. He was in Charlie's office for twelve minutes . . . then, he left the office, and the hotel. Charlie did not leave with him. The visitor taped a note to Charlie's door."

"That's it!" Frederick shouted. "Now I know why there was something about that note that didn't seem right. That wasn't my uncle's handwriting."

They took off, running towards Charlie's office. Frederick's long legs moved him yards ahead of the officers who were burdened with the weight of their gun belt and heavy bullet proof vests. Frederick arrived at Charlie's door and ripped off the note. "I'm positive – that isn't my uncle's handwriting."

Frederick put his ear against the door and listened. "I don't hear anything."

"Do you have a key to this door?" asked one of the policemen.

"No, not with me. It's back at the front desk."

"Stand back," said Sargent Franco. Fortunately, it was a cheap wooden door that broke apart after three forceful kicks, splintering the door. Frederick flipped on the light.

There was Charlie's motionless body slumped over at his desk, bound and gagged.

Forty-Seven

"This is Frederick," he firmly announced into his radio. "Charles Hamilton has been found. I repeat: Charles Hamilton has been found. Security, ask the hotel doctor to come to Mr. Hamilton's office, and call for an ambulance. Code Orange. I repeat, Code Orange," he said into the radio. Code Orange was a message to all personnel that the lobby needed to be cleared of all guests, the driveway up and around the front of the hotel cleared of all vehicles, and all hands on deck, as needed.

While Frederick made his radio call, the police officers quickly put on latex gloves. They ripped off the tape across Charlie's mouth, and used a pocket knife to cut the cable ties. "Frederick, don't touch anything," commanded one of the officers.

As Frederick reflected on the possibility that he would inherit his uncle's position one day, he wondered if he could handle the responsibilities of running the estate. A sudden appreciation of his uncle's abilities overwhelmed Frederick, and his eyes began to tear.

He had to be in charge now, and act responsibly. He gently asked inquiring guests and staff to move aside. He asked Manny at the front desk to bring stanchions from the lobby, and set them up to keep people at bay.

The hotel doctor, who lived on the premises, took charge. He checked Charlie's vitals. EMS arrived minutes later with a stretcher and other equipment.

"Your uncle is a very lucky man," the doctor whispered to Frederick. "Another few hours or so, we might have had a different outcome. His vitals are weak, but I'm sure a day or two in hospital will have him as good as new."

"Your uncle would be proud of you, Frederick," Franco said. "You did a fine job taking charge, organizing the search party, and staying calm. I'll be sure to tell Charlie how impressed we were."

"Gee, thanks," he said.

Frederick knew that if he didn't get to his room in another minute, he would start to cry in front of everyone. And he didn't want *that* getting back to Charles Hamilton VI.

Forty-Eight

Despite her objections, Simone was taken to Norwalk Hospital for a CT Scan of her head, as well as a physical exam. After receiving a clean bill of health, other than being told to "get some rest," she and Jennifer drove to Greenwich Hospital at five o'clock a.m. to see Charlie. He was still groggy from the powerful drug, but he was able to smile at the two women.

"Don't talk," she said, "I'm fine."

The attending doctor entered. "Will he be okay? When can I take him home?" Simone asked anxiously.

"Are you immediate family?"

"No, I'm not. I'm his girlfriend." The question hit Simone, her eyes filling with tears, as she answered.

"I'm sorry. I can't give you any information about his condition."

Charlie tried speaking, but the doctor told him to rest. "Let's go into the hallway, ladies."

The two women followed the doctor, hoping he would go against his principles, and give Simone a full update on Charlie's condition.

"I hope you understand that I cannot give someone claiming to be his girlfriend an update on his medical condition. Once his next of kin arrives, they'll make the decision as to whom can be informed of his health. I'm sorry, ladies. I have to get back to my rounds." The doctor turned, his white coat releasing a faint smell of antiseptic hand cleanser.

Like two guardians, they sat silently on uncomfortable plastic chairs, nestled in the corner of Charlie's room. The women occasionally nodded off, getting some much needed sleep. They awoke to the sounds of Charles Hamilton Senior roaring, "What's going on here?" His wife, was close behind.

"Shh!" Simone whispered, startling the parents. His father whipped around, and saw Simone and Jennifer keeping vigil. "He's sleeping," Jennifer added.

"I knew he would end up in trouble because of you," his father blared at Simone. "I want some answers." He charged out of the room, and headed toward the nurses' station, shouting as he walked, "I want to speak to the person in charge of my son."

Charlie's mother looked demurely at the two women, and apologized for her husband's outburst.

"No need to say anything. I understand," Simone whispered.

"Mom?" mumbled Charlie, his eyes barely opened. "Mom?" His mother ran to his bedside and held his hand. She kissed his cheek, and Simone saw a tear streaming down his face. Simone and Jennifer quietly slipped out of the room. They headed toward the cafeteria, in the opposite direction of Mr. Hamilton's ranting.

They walked in silence until they reached the food court. Here, they shared a stale bagel with frozen-hard butter, and cups of hot coffee.

"Jennifer, thank you for staying with me. I'm sorry if I've been preoccupied for several months. Hopefully, now my life will resume some normalcy."

"Did you ever suspect Jonathan?" Jennifer asked, taking a cautious sip of her hot beverage.

"No, not at all. Not even once."

Jennifer paused for a long moment. "I did," she admitted.

Simone turned and stared into Jennifer's eyes. Reeling from this admission, she asked, "Why didn't you say something? All of this might have been avoided." After a few seconds, she added, "I'm sorry, that's not fair. I shouldn't have said that."

Jennifer remained silent. She turned her eyes away from Simone's. It was too painful to see her partner and friend experience such grief.

"What made you suspicious?"

Jennifer slowly began to tell her story. "Well, I began doing some of my own investigative work. I was going to tell you about my findings, but then we had that spat before you left for Charlottesville. I know . . . I was probably getting even. But what I found out, I didn't think, related to someone coming into your house."

Jennifer continued, "I found out that Jonathan's nephew isn't his nephew at all, but his son. He's not married to the mother, but he supports her, financially. She got pregnant by another man, and Jonathan went nuts. He slapped her around, and she had him arrested, and obtained a protection order against him. His court date was December 18th, the same day as your party. That's why he had to see if he could attend. Apparently, the restraining order prevented him from seeing his son. Maybe that's why he put up the photograph, so he could 'see' his son anytime he was at work. He hired a defense attorney, and two weeks ago, the boy's mother dropped the charges. He can now see his son with supervised visitation. Obviously, that's a moot point, now," she added.

Simone was shocked by this information, and wondered what made Jennifer do this investigation.

"How do you know all this, Jennifer?"

"Well, you probably don't want to know, but Anthony's father knows a guy, who knows a guy. They snooped around."

Simone grimaced. "You're right. I don't want to know. But why did you investigate Jonathan in the first place?"

Jennifer went back to her story. "When we were waiting for our flight back home from Paris, Jonathan went into a duty-free gift shop at the airport. I went to the ladies room, but it was being cleaned, so I decided to go back to Jonathan, and try the restroom again later. I saw him in the store, purchasing a cell phone. I thought that was odd. He took the phone out of the package, and used it. Then, the strangest thing happened."

"What?" asked Simone, her anger mounting for not revealing this sooner.

"He left the store, and headed towards the men's room."

"What's so strange about that?" Simone asked. "And, didn't he see you?"

"Well, because I thought it was suspicious . . . him buying a phone . . . I hid behind a pillar. He didn't see me. So I followed him toward the restrooms. I saw him discretely drop the phone into the trash can, before he entered the bathroom."

Simone used all her energy to control her temper. "Jennifer, I can't believe you didn't tell me this earlier. I received a text while I was in Paris with Charlie, shortly after he arrived. He read it, and it caused a huge fight."

"I'm sorry, Simone. You said you got a text or two, but you didn't say anything after you returned from Paris. I assumed that after I received the information about Jonathan's son, that he probably used the phone to text him. It's cheaper than buying a Sim card to make international calls from your personal phone. I just never thought of telling you."

"What he used in the airport was called a burner phone - the kind you throw away after using it. The same type of phone used to send me text messages."

"Oh."

Simone continued, her voice rising. "But that still doesn't answer the question why you felt the need to do a background check on him."

"When Barbara told us that Biff was killed because someone ordered cookies - possibly from the hotel lobby - I thought back to the night we came home after midnight from touring Paris. Jonathan said he saw the woman who checked us in, and wanted to talk to her. But I didn't see her at the counter, did you?"

"Come to think of it, no. I assumed he saw her and that she had walked into the office for a moment."

"Since I didn't see her, I thought Jonathan mixed her up with another woman at the counter. But then the phone call from the lobby . . . and the timing . . . it just made me suspicious. And because you got upset that I made decisions on my own about the phone messages I returned, I wasn't going to tell you the results of the background check that I did, a decision I made on my own."

Simone got up from the table and walked to the windows. Fresh snow had started falling over Greenwich, covering the grass and trees, leaving the roadways wet. Fresh anger fell over Simone, along with confusion, betrayal, and a bit of foolishness.

The doctor on call found Simone and called to her, "Ms. Simpson."

She turned, trying to read his face. "What is it? Is Charlie okay?"

"He's asking for you."

Simone followed him, not turning around to look at Jennifer.

She rushed into Charlie's room. He was sitting up, more alert, and a huge transformation from half an hour earlier.

"Simone," he whispered. "I can't talk, my throat hurts."

"That's fine. I'll do all the talking for a change." They smiled at each other lovingly.

"I'm sorry I yelled at you, Simone," his father said apologetically from the other side of the bed. "This event caused a major scare for our family. I never thought . . ."

"Dear," Charlie's mother said softly. "How about we give our son some privacy." Charlie's father morphed into a little boy, nodded, and followed his wife out of the room.

"Charlie, I'm so sorry this happened to you. I'm still in disbelief that Jonathan would do such a thing to you."

"Are you okay, Simone? Did Jonathan hurt you?" his raspy voice straining.

She paused for a long moment before telling him. "I killed him, Charlie. I've never killed anyone in my life, but it was either him or me."

Simone rested her head on Charlie's chest, the pain on the right side of her face resurfacing, reminding her of the events. He tried putting his hand on her back, but the intravenous needle pinned inside his vein, prevented any movement.

With a raspy voice, he whispered, "It'll be okay, my love. No more fears, no more break-ins, no more texts. You're finally free from all of that."

The doctor arrived again. Simone grabbed a handful of tissues from the tiny box next to Charlie's bed. She blew her nose so loudly, they all laughed.

"Be careful young lady. You might set off some alarms with that nose," the doctor quipped.

"I have some good news, Charlie. You can be discharged. You'll need to rest for a week or more. You'll have burns on your wrists from the cable ties for a few more days, and your skin will feel raw when you shave. Other than that, you won't have any restrictions," he said.

"Ms. Simpson, your friend Jennifer said that she was going home. She said something about not going back to your house, and you'll be staying with Charlie. Something about it being a crime scene. She was rather upset while she spoke to me, so I only got part of the story.

In any case, she seems to have abandoned you here. If you need a cab, let me know."

Simone whispered, "Thanks. I'm fine."

The doctor left the room.

What's that all about?" Charlie asked.

"A story for another time. Now, we need to get you dressed, and back to the hotel. We'll order room service."

Charlie moaned at the thought of eating greasy fries for breakfast. But at this moment, all he cared about was knowing that Simone was safe, and back in his arms.

Forty-Nine

Simone and Charlie left on December 23rd for her apartment on Rue des Barres in Paris. As they promised their doctors, they rested, slept late, and took advantage of the city's soothing energy.

Mrs. Smith and Irene arrived in Paris on December 15th, and planned to stay until the end of January. The two women worked tirelessly, and prepared Judy's apartment for her visit. Irene was pleased to discover a small maid's room with her own bath.

Judy and Harold had gotten engaged after Thanksgiving, and were now living in Judy's spacious apartment in Richmond. They would arrive on the 20th, returning to the States on January 2nd.

Earlier that year, Harold had asked Mr. Smith for his daughter's hand in marriage. The two men discussed at length Harold's ambitions and financial stability. After all, Mr. Smith wasn't a fool. Several young men had come along wanting to marry the daughter of a successful and wealthy attorney; interested in marrying Judy's future inheritance, and not Judy. But Harold was different, thought Mr. Smith, and whole heartedly agreed to the impending engagement.

After Mr. Smith's sudden death, Harold put off asking Judy for her hand in marriage until November. He explained that he had talked to her father, and then to her mother, both of whom approved of the marriage, and welcomed him like a son. The couple planned to marry in the spring of the following year.

The sunny apartment overlooked the Seine. It was a large five bedroom, four bath apartment, filled with antiques. There weren't many changes Judy wanted to make – a few upgrades, like new mattresses and more modern appliances. Otherwise, it was perfect.

Judy had also been kept in the dark about her father owning the two penthouse apartments until after his death. She and her family had stayed there twice over the years, and Judy believed it belonged to one of her father's law partners. She never imagined it would become hers one day.

After Judy's suite was in order, Irene took charge of airing out, and cleaning Simone's apartment, equally as large and sunny. It wasn't used very often, so it was in need of many repairs. That would be a mission Charlie and Simone would take on with pleasure.

By the time the couple arrived, Simone's apartment was cleaned with fresh linens on the bed, and a vase of fresh flowers (not roses) on the kitchen table. Irene roasted a chicken nestled on root vegetables, which she left in the refrigerator for Charlie and Simone's arrival. She and Mrs. Smith then went to the market and purchased sundries.

Irene promised a delicious dinner for Christmas Eve. She needed to cook some of the vegetables in Simone's oven, because the one in Judy's apartment, "Isn't as big as what we have back home. But I'll manage," Irene countered.

Aromas of homemade pie and roast turkey filled the hallways of the building. Even the elevator operator commented, "You must be having one big feast up there."

"Yes," Simone said. "I believe my mother is overdoing it a bit." She never called Mrs. Smith 'mother' and now that she did, her throat got thick with emotion. Rather, she often referred to Mr. Smith as her adopted father. Mrs. Smith was like a mother to her, coming to her aid at all the crucial moments in her adult life.

Irene didn't disappoint. Christmas dinner was indeed a feast, starting with fresh shucked oysters nestled on crushed ice.

"They're abundant," chimed Mrs. Smith.

Irene turned her nose up to them, and refused to even try one. "They took me an hour to open. My hands are raw. And that's about the only thing I want raw."

They all laughed as they devoured the delicious delicacies.

The next course was foie gras. Again, Irene rejected the delicacy. "I've cooked duck, but usually gave the liver to the dogs."

"They don't know how good they have it," Harold said.

Words like, 'yum,' and, 'this is so delicious,' were uttered among the appreciative diners. Of course, you can't be in France and not wash down your meal with Champagne. Over the course of the evening, they consumed three bottles of the expensive elixir, feeling slightly inebriated.

The main course was a golden brown turkey. "I ain't seen nothing like it," Irene said. "Missus and I went to the meat market, and full birds were hanging on hooks. I've skinned and cleaned my share of fowl in my life, but I thought those days were over," she giggled after giving out a slight belch. "Oh, excuse me. How unladylike," They roared with laughter.

"Have some more champagne," said Charlie, teasing Irene.

The final part of the meal presented a variety of cheeses. "I'm told you can't have a meal without some fine cheese," said Irene, as she spread a water cracker with Chevre.

"That's correct, Irene," Simone agreed. "No good Frenchman finishes a meal without some aged cheese. It goes great with champagne," she teased the housekeeper as she refilled the woman's glass.

"Oh no! No more of the devil's liquid for me. Soon, I'll be snoring at the table."

Mrs. Smith reached over and took Irene's hand in hers. "You know, my friend, I don't believe we've ever shared a meal together. After all the years you've been with my family, I don't remember a time you joined Henry and me. We've certainly devoured your delicious meals. It's only right that you should join us."

"I know my place, Missus. It's a great honor to sit here with you and your daughter. And her fine, handsome man. Thank you."

"More champagne, Irene?" teased Charlie.

She tossed her cloth napkin at him. "Beast! Miss Simone, you've got to watch him. I think he wants to get me drunk so he can have his way with me."

"He's all mine!" Simone teased.

The final course was Irene's attempt at a bûche de Noël. "It looks a little lopsided," Judy said, "but it is delicious."

"Logs are analogous to people," Harold pontificated. "Each one is shaped differently with varying colors, shapes and textures. A log, like a person, can be strong, rough, or weak.

"That's very philosophical," said Mrs. Smith.

"It's the champagne," chimed in Irene, introducing more laughter to those gathered at the feast.

Charlie lifted his fork, and used it to clink his wine glass to get everyone's attention. "I have an announcement to make."

Everyone stopped talking, as Charlie stood up, and removed a sheaf of paper from his pocket.

"What is it, Charlie?" Simone asked.

"This, ladies and gentleman, are my final divorce papers. I'm finally free."

"Oh, how wonderful . . . that's great." Everyone applauded.

"When did this happen?" Mrs. Smith asked.

"I received the final papers on December 10th, but wanted to wait until now to announce the good news. It's been a long time coming, and I'm happy that all the negative people are out of our lives. Eve announced she's moving to horse country in Pennsylvania with her latest beau, and Simone's stalker is out of our lives."

"Let's have some more champagne," Judy suggested as she refilled Irene's glass, without any resistance from the housekeeper.

"A splendid idea," Irene shouted.

Glasses were refilled and lifted in honor of Charlie's good news.

"Here's to a future of happiness," Mrs. Smith said. She knew she was seeing the beginning of a new chapter unfolding in Simone's life.

Then Charlie turned to Simone, got down on one knee, pulled a small box from his pocket, and asked, "Simone Deschamps Simpson, will you marry me?"

The answer was evident.

www.ingramcontent.com/pod-product-compliance
Lightning Source LLC
Chambersburg PA
CBHW061142170626
46809CB00003B/957